THE PAINTER'S APPRENTICE

A YA Portal Fantasy

Alexander Small

Alexander Small Publishing

Copyright © 2021 Alexander Small

All rights reserved

The Painter's Apprentice is a work of fiction. Any similarity to real persons, living or dead, is coincidental and not intended by the author.

No part of this book may be reproduced, or stored in a retrieval system, or transmitted in any form or by any means, electronic, mechanical, photocopying, recording, or otherwise, without express written permission of the publisher.

ISBN-13: 9798503229233

Library of Congress Control Number: 2018675309
Printed in the United States of America

Creating a novel is always a challenging task. This is even more the case when you're moving into a new genre. This wasn't my first novel, but it was my first attempt at writing Young Adult fiction. I couldn't have done it without the encouragement and support of some wonderful friends.

Bearing that in mind, I'd like to thank the following people:

Cathy Andrews for her excellent editing work.

Marissa Schimdt for alpha reading with impeccable eyes.

Taylor Aston White for all her fantastic help with marketing, and so much more.

Rebecca Eiseman, Ash St John and Linda Chalmers for always being such eager and skilled beta readers.

Molly Zenk for giving incredibly helpful guidance on everything book-related you could imagine.

A NOTE ON LANGUAGE

This novel is written in UK English. That means the language--including spelling and punctuation--within The Painter's Apprentice will differ in some ways from novels written in US English. Please bear this in mind while reading.

The author respectfully asks any queries about book content or general feedback be directed to him personally, rather than the book outlet you purchased your copy from.

Please feel free to get in touch with Alexander via email at: alexandersmallauthor@gmail.com

The painting has a life of its own. I try to let it come through.

JACKSON POLLOCK

CONTENTS

Title Page
Copyright
Dedication
A Note on language
Epigraph
Contents — 1
Chapter 1 — 2
Chapter 2 — 9
Chapter 3 — 14
Chapter 4 — 20
Chapter 5 — 31
Chapter 6 — 42
Chapter 7 — 48
Chapter 8 — 56
Chapter 9 — 63
Chapter 10 — 70
Chapter 11 — 81

Chapter 12	93
Chapter 13	100
Chapter 14	108
Chapter 15	121
Chapter 16	123
Chapter 17	134
Chapter 18	138
Chapter 19	153
Chapter 20	161
Chapter 21	169
Chapter 22	177
Chapter 23	185
Chapter 24	208
Chapter 25	215
Chapter 26	226
Chapter 27	234
Chapter 28	247
Chapter 29	253
Chapter 30	261
Chapter 31	269
Chapter 32	275
Chapter 33	278
Chapter 34	282
Chapter 35	292

Chapter 36	299
Chapter 37	304
Epilogue	306
About The Author	317
A Note on reviews from the author	319
Sequel	321

CONTENTS

Chapter 1
Chapter 2
Chapter 3
Chapter 4
Chapter 5
Chapter 6
Chapter 7
Chapter 8
Chapter 9
Chapter 10
Chapter 11
Chapter 12
Chapter 13
Chapter 14
Chapter 15
Chapter 16
Chapter 17
Chapter 18
Chapter 19
Chapter 20
Chapter 21
Chapter 22
Chapter 23
Chapter 24
Chapter 25

Chapter 26
Chapter 27
Chapter 28
Chapter 29
Chapter 30
Chapter 31
Chapter 32
Chapter 33
Chapter 34
Chapter 35
Chapter 36
Chapter 37
Epilogue

CHAPTER 1

The smash of glass is hard to sleep through. Even more so when accompanied by shouting.

Sitting up in bed, Jack rubbed his eyes and listened. More smashing. Sounded like plates, cups, and glasses; their crashing chimes blending with bellows and yells.

Another argument. This one sounded more serious though. They didn't normally throw things.

Slabs of silvery hue stretched across superhero-themed bedsheets in a formation of four. Jack couldn't sleep without the sky's protective glow. Every night, his dad would draw the curtains tight, leaving him in darkness and telling him not to be such a scaredy cat. He'd wait until his dad's feet had made their final creak going down the stairs, then he'd sneak across the room and open them. He always got up earlier than both his parents, so nobody had any idea he remained frightened of the dark. It was one of many charades to be found in their home.

The biggest of which was their contented family life. His parents' public smiles and affectionate gestures gave way to scowling eyes, snide remarks and shouting matches in private. Tension was never absent, even when things seemed ok. It crisscrossed the air like invisible spider webs, waiting to ensnare.

And it certainly had tonight. Usually, whenever the chatter of venomous insults slithered up the stairs, Jack's normal reaction would be to plug ears with fingers and fade into slumber. This time was different though. There was no way he could sleep through that racket. He wondered what had caused such heated rage. Words were now accompanied by weapons—probably thrown by his mum—and he felt an irresistible draw to hear what was going on.

Pulling back the covers, he walked towards the door, grasping, and rolling its smooth wooden handle until he heard a familiar metallic click. Easing it open—mindful of the hinges' mild squeak—he crept and crouched beside the bannister, peering with caution between pillars of varnished wood. Not close enough. Their house had three floors and he would need to creep to the next landing to hear their conversation clearly.

So down he sneaked, thankful his slight

frame didn't cause the aging planks to croak his presence like they did with his parents. Green carpet flowed down the stairs' middle, held in place by thin brass strips. Once luxuriant, its fraying, grubby fibres were coarse under the thin cotton socks on his feet. Nobody had taken care of it—or much else around the house—since the day his mum told the maid to leave.

The door to the kitchen was open. He couldn't see, but he could hear. Hiding behind the large corner part of the bannister, he listened.

"No wonder we're skint." His mum's voice was shrill, slurred, the words muddled. She'd been having her favourite drink again: pink gin. It turned her cheeks the same colour and smelled like sweet perfume. "I'm living like a scullery maid here. You think I couldn't go out and do better for myself? Eh?"

"Oh, shut up, ya drunken tart. Whose money do you think it is? I earn it, I'll do what I like with it. You've still got your gin and cigarettes, don't ya? Eh? Not short of them, are ya?" His dad spoke in a lower tone; the words were fast but firm.

"Shut up, Arthur"—Jack heard the rasp of a loosening bottle top and chink of glass on glass — "I think, it's our money. *Our* money. What little's left of it. Why do you think I married you? For your good looks and charm?" The final part of the question was stretched thin, ending with a cackle. "If I'd known you were gonna turn into a bloody degenerate gambler I would never have—"

"And why do you think I married you, eh? For your brains? Einstein,"—he heard his dad let out a snort— "always dazzling me with your intellectual conversation aren't ya?"

"I've got more brains than you, that's for sure. I don't throw my money away in those bloody casinos or at the bookies'. That's clever, isn't it? You're a bloody genius, Arthur. You should apply to Oxford."

"No, you drink your—correction *my*—money away instead. I married a beauty queen and now what have I got? A moaning old drunk for a wife."

"Old, is it? Old? I'm thirty-two, you idiot. You're practically a pensioner. You—"

"Look, Debs"—his dad let out a long sigh and then wood scraped across kitchen tiles— "you've had your little tantrum, now sit down and calm down. And, come on, don't have any more, for Christ's sake."

"Sod off"—Jack heard another rattle and clink— "I'll stop when I feel like it, not when you tell me to. I'm not one of your lackeys. Wanker."

"Have a seat and calm down. And—"

"Sod off, Arthur! You're nothing now. Just a sad, old man who doesn't have two pennies to rub together. And I think I might go and look for someone who knows how to keep a lady."

The crisp sound of a sharp slap was followed by shrieks and shattering glass. And then another slap. And another. His mum's crying echoed around the dimly lit hallway.

"Keep a lady? I've done nothing but keep you. I've given you everything, ya cow. And what have you given me? Eh? What have you ever given me?"

"I gave you a son," she answered, between sobs.

"What, Little Picasso? He's as useless as his bloody mum."

There was wooden clatter—a drawer or cupboard being yanked open—and the silvery rustle of steel. "Well, you know what they say about apples and trees. Now you touch me again and see what happens." Her voice had steadied, sounding hard, angry.

"Put that down, you stupid cow. You're gonna get hurt."

"You stay away from me, you bloody animal. I should never have got involved with you lot. Bunch of bloody thugs, the lot of you."

"Well, you're the one waving a knife around, Deborah."

"I know what you're capable of, remember?"

"You better watch your mouth. Now give me that—"

"Keep away from me!"

"I said give me it you—"

He heard the scrape and smack of wood,

another smash, and then his dad shouting. "You bitch!"

There was a scream which ended in muffle. More wooden groans, objects knocking, glass rattling. Then silence.

His grip on the bannister had been getting ever tighter—to the point of clamping—but now it was sliding on the smooth surface. Palms soaked and mouth parched, he was frozen. Until the top of his dad's head appeared from the kitchen door only one flight underneath where Jack was perched. He had a dish towel wrapped around his hand and was muttering curses through deep gasps of breath. And he was coming up the stairs.

Jack put every cat in the neighbourhood to shame. Nimble, floating like his feet were feather dusters, he raced in Superman socks and silence. Easing the bedroom door closed—the squeak even more vital to avoid—he dived into bed, pulling the sheets around him; hoping closed eyes and false sleep would ward off whatever was coming.

The stairs sounded his dad's approach; each creak causing Jack's body to tense further. His dad was on the landing below now, climbing further with steady steps. And that was when Jack realised the curtains were still open. Pulling back the covers, he pounced. The curtain railing had a slight whistle to it, so he had to draw them with both care and speed in mind.

Hearing the final stair bending with pressure, he fumbled the last shard of light closed. Then he slid into bed and wrapped the blanket neck high with precision that would have made ninjas envious. Pretending to sleep while his heart pulsed from toe to throat, he kept his eyes closed but fought the urge to screw them shut.

The door clicked open softly. "Jack." The word was whispered. The door squeaked a little and he got the feeling his dad was standing just inside the doorway. Of course, he didn't dare open his eyes to see. "Jack, you awake son?" The volume was raised, but not by much.

Never more awake in his life. And never more asleep.

The door was closed with a tiny squeak and click.

CHAPTER 2

It was the morning after his parents' big argument.

The good news was he didn't have to go to school. The bad news was his mother had run away to America. They'd had a big disagreement, then she'd packed her bags and been picked up by her American friends, so his dad was telling him.

There definitely had been visitors in the night. Being unable to sleep—kept awake by a blend of adrenaline and frightening darkness—he'd heard the rasp of exhaust and rumbling crunch of tires on their gravel driveway. Car doors had been opened and shut, the pop and clamp of a boot too. The wisps of conversation were too distant and hurried to make sense of, but the accents had all sounded English. Not any American ones, like on TV.

Now Jack was sitting on one of the living room couches. His dad was hunched forward on the edge of his favourite armchair. The tan seat gave off tiny leather squeaks as he shuffled, adjusting from a stiff perch, to reclining and then back again. One hand was wrapped in cream-coloured bandage, a patch of dark red staining the part which covered his palm. The pale fingers of his other hand pinched and tapped at the chair's thick, faded arms. A glass almost full of amber liquid sat on the small circular table beside him; the type of glass that looked like a mini goldfish bowl on a stem and broad stand.

His dad didn't usually drink that stuff. He said it made you say and do stupid things. But now he was having it for breakfast. Jack could smell the powerful vapours coming from his dad's lips as he spoke. They were like cinnamon and dried-up old fruit. Why did grownups like that stuff?

"Look, son"—he took another large slurp from the glass, its contents swirling and knocking the sides as he placed it down again— "your mother. She"—he blew a popped puff which stretched into a heavy sigh— "she wasn't happy. Not happy at all, in fact. She always had dreams of being an actress, in Hollywood, you know like on the telly and all that."

"But she never even said goodbye," said Jack with a tone that made it more complaint than statement. He wanted to say more but was wary of his dad's mood swings.

Pock-marked cheeks bunching and lips pursing, his dad nodded rapidly. "I know, Jack. I know. Believe me, and that hurts even more than this"—he held up his bandaged hand with the palm outwards— "to think she was so angry she didn't even say goodbye to her own son."

Blood was seeping through. It looked wet. The cut must have been bad.

"What happened?" He didn't like to ask questions of his dad—as it made him angry—but he sensed it was a day of special privileges.

Jack's dad took another mouthful of the strong-smelling drink and let out a sigh and chuckle. "Well, putting it mildly, your dear old mum had—has—a bit of a temper on her. I'm afraid she threw one or two things around before she left with her mates. I cut myself cleaning up one of the broken glasses off the floor. Silly old me, eh?"

His chestnut brown hair was normally combed flat and slick with shiny gel, parted to the side in a sharp dividing line. Now it was unkempt and dry, like bristles on a scrubbing brush. His trimmed moustache was still perfectly groomed though, as if pencilled on. It was unusual to see it sitting above a sympathetic smile. Jack was only accustomed to disapproving grunts, frowns and glares; his father's mild manner was making him uneasy.

"Do you think she'll come back?" Jack asked.

He felt a film of sweat on his forehead, the neckline of his t-shirt was damp. Either the heating was turned up too high or he was sick from worry and lack of sleep.

Shaking his head and sucking in air through gritted teeth, his dad replied, "I think its best we move on, son. I don't think we'll be seeing her again. Although I hope, really hope"—he lightly pressed his hands in a praying motion— "that I'm wrong, of course. Hope she realizes her mistake and comes back."

"I hope so too." Jack had a horrible feeling hope wouldn't help.

"Good lad. Now"—his dad leaned forward and beckoned with his bandaged hand for Jack to do the same— "what's important is, if anyone at school—say for example a classmate, or that nosey old cow Mrs Thompson—asks where your mum is, you say she's gone off to America, ok?"

Their faces were only inches apart. He could see every detail of his father's eyeballs. Gleaming marbles criss-crossed with scarlet slivers, their hazel centres were piercing, focused. The spice from his breath made Jack want to wipe his eyes.

"Yes, dad."

His uninjured hand grasped Jack's bony shoulder, the fingertips pressing, rubbing hard as his voice lowered, close to a whisper. "And you can never tell anyone about your mum being angry, or if we ever had arguments, or using nasty words, or throwing stuff, and especially me having this"—he gestured to the bandage with his eyes— "or people might get the wrong idea. And that could cause big problems for both of us. Is that clear?"

"Yes, dad."

His dad gave him a sharp shake. Speech slowing, he knocked out words solid as rocks. "I said, is that clear?"

Jack's shoulder was starting to hurt a little. "Yes, dad."

"Ok. Now, someone asks you where your mum's gone. What do you say?"

"She's gone off to America. She wants to be on the TV."

"Good boy," he said with a softening voice and thin smile. The—now painful—grip was released as his dad sat back in the chair and took a gulp from the glass, releasing a gasp of satisfaction. "Ok, you've got the day off from school. I'll write you a sick note. Why don't you go and do some of your drawings? You like that, don't you?"

"Yes, dad. Can I have some toast?"

"Course you can. And you're old enough to make your own breakfast now. Don't ask me. Off you go and help yourself." Fishing into his jean pocket, he took out his phone and began swiping and tapping, staring at the screen while he sipped at his drink. Without looking up he mumbled, "Go on then. Off you pop, Little Picasso."

CHAPTER 3

Looking through his bedroom's open sash window with its frame coated in cracked and peeling white paint, Jack smiled at the summer scene in front of him. Their—admittedly overgrown—lawn was blanketed in mesmerising golden beams. Contented warble drifted from beaks amongst the branches of trees lining the gravel drive to their house. A lukewarm breeze was washing in, causing the drawing under his fingers to flutter and flap as he layered, scribbled, refined and defined.

Months had passed since his mum had disappeared, and the sun was soothing bruised memories. Chirping birds were cheering him up. As were the six weeks' summer holidays which had started the day before. six whole weeks away from school, to draw whatever he liked.

Jack only had ordinary pencils, but he was

still transforming plain paper into a bountiful summer garden, bursting with life. For those with the imagination to appreciate it, of course.

A knock interrupted. He knew it wasn't his dad because he just came straight in. "Yes, come in."

The door squeaked and a familiar face poked round. "Alright, Jack. Mind if I come in?" It was one of his dad's mates. His name was Henderson, but everyone called him Hendy. Jack liked Hendy. Or rather, he found him far less scary than the dozen other men his dad was friends with. Plus, Hendy was always laughing and making jokes and he never scowled at Jack.

His mum hadn't liked him at all. Once, during one of his parents' countless arguments, she'd called Hendy a vicious rottweiler. He didn't understand that. The family at the bottom of the road had a rottweiler and it was nice. It barked a bit but if you whispered and petted it, it was friendly.

"Sure, Hendy. I'm drawing the garden."

He plodded in with a smile, and stood beside Jack, catching the sun's honey hues. Jack wasn't sure what was shinier: his shoes or his head. Hendy wasn't overly tall—about normal, like his dad—but his upper body was like two men glued together. And the smart suit jacket he wore was stretched tight over bulging arms, big as the wrestlers on TV. Chin stubbled, ears studded, and forehead wrinkled, he was his dad's closest—and biggest—friend. He even said cheeky things to his dad that Jack wouldn't have dared.

Peering at the drawing, Hendy twitched his eyebrows and blew out a soft whistle of admiration. His voice was deep, strained, like the muscles in his stumpy neck wouldn't let the words come out properly. "Blimey, you're something, ain't you, Jack? Can I have a look?" His aftershave was a mix of coconuts—but not fresh ones—and something like baby powder and lemon. Jack wasn't a fan.

He handed him the drawing. "It's not finished yet, but I think it's going well."

Hendy's lips parted to reveal gaps and gold. "Going very well, I should say. Here, you can show it to your dad. He wants to talk with you, about your artistic skills in fact."

"Really?"

With a soft tut and eye roll he replied, "Yes really. Now come on, get a move on, you cheeky little sausage." He ruffled Jack's raven hair with a calloused palm that covered his whole crown.

Clasping his work, he padded down the stairs with Hendy's bulky frame lumbering close behind.

In the living room, his dad was sitting—as usual—in the same tan leather armchair, staring at his phone screen. Hair immaculate, he was wearing a beige suit, white shirt and gold tie. His suede brown shoes were the kind that didn't need laces. A cup of coffee sat on the table beside him; bitter, herby vapours were rising from the liquid's black surface. Jack liked the smell but had tried a sip once and hated the strong flavour. Adults had strange tastes.

Standing over by the bay window, leaning on the windowsill and looking out into the garden, was another of his dad's friends. A guy called Ramon. Dressed in a drab grey suit, he was skinny for a grownup, or maybe he just looked that way compared to Hendy. In any case, his face was narrow, the nose pointed and sharp. He was the only one of his dad's friends who didn't have a moustache, beard or stubble. He looked like a clean-shaven ferret. Or rat. Ramon always talked about Jack like he wasn't there, and if Jack said hi, he only gave a sneer or grunt. Yea, Jack didn't like Ramon much.

Hendy walked over to his dad and laid Jack's drawing on the chair's arm. "Some talent your boy's got. Have a look."

Looking up from his phone screen, his dad held the paper in both hands, it crinkled between his fingers as he scanned it, making mumbling "Mhm" noises. Compliments were rare from his dad. Non-existent, in fact.

Today was different though. Nodding and smiling, he stroked his moustache and said, "Yea. Yea that's excellent that is. Looks like a master in the making." Hendy gave Jack a wink before sitting on the old-style couch in the corner. Its springs sang out rusty creaks of complaint under the weight.

Then his dad spoke to him. "Jack, you love art, don't you?" He took a sip of the coffee, placing it back on its saucer with a gentle clink.

"Yes, dad."

"And you don't like school, do you?"

"Not really." His dad knew these answers, so why was he asking?

"Why doesn't he like school?" asked Ramon from across the room. His squeaky voice matched his features.

Annoyance flashed across his dad's face as he turned round in his chair to answer the question. "That's not important right now, so would you put a sock in it?"

Holding out two palms in a defensive gesture, Ramon replied, "Alright, Arthur. Sorry."

Returning to meet Jack's eyes, he said, "Now what if instead of school, you could spend all day doing art, with no other kids to get on your nerves? Just learning to be even better at drawing —and other kinds of art—than you already are. Would you like that?"

"Yes, dad, I would." It seemed like a bad joke. Except he noticed how his dad and Hendy were dressed. Everything pressed crisp, polished and shiny. Like they were going to a wedding or a big business meeting.

"That's great then, son. Cause guess what? Two weeks ago, I sent off one of your drawings to a competition. An incredibly special competition, in fact. Now"—he sipped from the coffee again, giving a small of gasp of satisfaction— "I didn't expect to hear anything back. I mean, I might call you Little Picasso sometimes, but that doesn't make it so does it? So—"

"What—"

His dad's tone solidified; the eyebrows lowered. "I haven't finished talking."

"Sorry, dad." Curiosity was making Jack careless.

"So, long story short, I did hear back. With an invite from the bloke who holds the competition. An Italian painter called Dante De Luca, who's always on the look out for an apprentice. Every two years he accepts examples from talented kids such as yourself and—if he likes what he sees—he invites the hopefuls up to do a piece of art for him. And if that art is good enough, then Bob's your uncle, they've won an apprenticeship. Apparently, he's done it for the past thirty odd years. And do you know how many apprentices he's chosen in all that time?"

Jack hesitated, double-checking his dad was expecting an answer, before answering. "How many?"

"None."

CHAPTER 4

Later that same morning, they boarded a train to Scotland. That was where Dante De Luca lived. Far up in the highlands.

His dad had stuffed two sets of clothes, spare trainers and a toothbrush into Jack's school rucksack before Ramon dropped them all off at the station with their luggage.

Now they were sitting in a large private compartment in one of the first-class carriages; him, his dad and Hendy. Looking through the window, he leaned a forearm on the smooth wooden central table and watched houses, hills and trees whizzing by. He liked the rhythmic click and clack of the tracks and the soft felt seat against his back. This was Jack's first time on a train, and it was interesting.

Hendy's chunky legs were spread over two seats, on Jack's side. He'd been to the restaurant carriage and came back with a bunch of goodies. Including a big chocolate bar and lemonade for Jack.

His dad was sat across the table from Jack. He'd been staring at the invitation letter for half an hour. Smirking to himself and nodding, he was looking at the ceiling, daydreaming.

"Twenty-five grand. Twenty-five—win or lose—just for taking part. Can you believe that? And I get an extra five grand for travel expenses. Five! I know this De Luca fella is bloody minted, but to be throwing cash around like that. I dunno, what is it with these people, eh? More money than sense," said his dad, folding the letter and slipping it inside his jacket.

Hendy opened a can of beer with a crack and hiss, sucking at the thick brown foam as it bubbled out of the freshly punctured hole. Smelled like chopped flowers mixed with dark chocolate. Tilting the can, he took a long guzzle before wiping his mouth on the back of his meaty hand. "Well,"—he belched beer gas— "probably sells a lot of paintings and that, doesn't he?"

His dad's sleek phone was laid on the table. He picked it up and gently shook the slender silver rectangle in Hendy's direction. "That's the funny thing. Been reading up on Mr De Luca. Strange geezer, reclusive. Can't even find a photo of him online. Only seems to sell a handful of paintings every decade, on average. And never at auction. Only to select clients."

"Does he get a lot for them then?" he asked before taking another mouthful.

His dad gave a snort. "A lot? Have a guess what his last painting went for. You get it right first time, I'll buy you six more of those," he said with a smug smile, gesturing to the beer can.

"Well"—he shrugged, glugged and swirled beer in thought— "I dunno, let's say ten million?"

"You ain't even close, my old son. Go on, I'll give you another guess. On the house."

"Alright, then. Hundred million."

He scoffed. "Still nowhere close. His last painting went for five hundred million quid." His dad left a gap of a second between each word, to add weight to the statement.

Hendy sat up, putting his beer on the table. "You must be joking. Who would pay that for a stupid bloody painting?"

"Bloody hell should I know. Some mug with too much money. But—according to the papers —that's what it went for. So, when we're up there, best behaviour ok? This bloke is richer than the queen. You never know what opportunities might present themselves. Plus, you never know"—he looked across at Jack with raised eyebrows— "Little Picasso here might even win."

The journey continued. Hendy swigged, burped and snoozed; his dad swiped and tapped. Jack cracked and munched squares of silky milk chocolate and enjoyed the landscapes. The train whirred past sun-soaked fields of lush green and golden yellow. Idyllic cottages and farms replaced concrete blocks and tarmac; their walls washed brilliant white and topped in sumptuous terracotta. Hills and valleys were dotted with chubby sheep chewing their fill under skies soft blue, peppered with puffs of white. He was the only one who noticed the sign that said: Welcome to Scotland.

A short while after, Hendy leaned close; his massive shoulder was bigger than Jack's head. "How's the, uh, chocolate? Any good?"

Jack ran his fingernail over the paper and foil to find the groove between the bar's blocks and snapped a strip off for Hendy. "Yea, it's good. Try some."

"Oh, don't mind if I do. Thank you very much."

"We're in Scotland now," said Jack.

With the whole piece of four blocks shoved in his mouth at once, Hendy was almost talking a foreign language when he replied, "Fought I smelt something."

Hendy chuckled; His dad sniggered, saying, "Scottish poofs, poncing round with their skirts and bagpipes."

Once he'd finished the chocolate, erasing the final traces with a circulating tongue, Hendy said, "So, what's this about school then? There a problem?"

"I—"

"He doesn't like school. Gets bullied. Don't

you?" His dad spoke with precise words and pitiless gaze.

"Oh, is that right?" Hendy reached into the paper bag from the restaurant carriage and pulled out another beer. He offered it to Jack's dad, who reacted with a tut and sideways head shake.

After making himself comfy in the corner seat, Hendy opened the can, drank, and blew a strong sigh, before saying, "School's a scary place sometimes, isn't it? Especially when you're not a big lad. But, Jack, you've got to stand up to bullies, or they'll just take more liberties. There'll come a point where you'll have to decide, believe you me. One day, you'll have to fight back. You know I went to school with your dad?" Jack shook his head. His dad had closed his phone and was focused on Hendy's words. "Yea, that's how we became mates. Met when we were—how old were we, Arthur?"

His dad did a brief upward eye search. "About eleven? Twelve? Little older than him."

"Yea, little squirts we were, like you." He tipped the can again, releasing a mini burp. "We had a bully at our school too. Can tell you a story about him if you like, Jack?"

Licking his lips and leaning into his seat, his dad replied on Jack's behalf with a thin smile. "Yea, go on then. Got plenty time to kill. I'm sure it'll be mostly bollocks the way you tell them, but if it passes the time."

Hendy winked at Jack. "Not bollocks at all. The God's honest truth. That's all you get from me."

"Ha! Course it is me old China. Anyway, go on then." His dad folded his arms, waiting for the story to start.

"So, anyway"—Hendy pinched the can's sides with fingers thick as pork sausages, causing crinkly tinkles— "you see those marks on your dad's cheeks?"

Jack nodded, hoping Hendy wouldn't say anything to cause upset.

"That's cause your dad had acne at school. When he was about twelve or so, he broke out into the worst acne you can imagine. You know what acne is?"

He shook his head.

Making a circular motion with his palm, he said, "Horrible red spots all over here. Your dad had that. And on his neck too. Looked like pepperoni pizza, it—"

"Watch it, will ya."

He took another gulp of beer and opened his mouth with stubbly cheeks bunched towards his eyes, as if to make a cheeky reply. His dad wasn't smiling. Hendy seemed to change his mind. "Well, anyway, your dad had skin issues, shall we say. And there was this boy. Shit"—he chuckled to himself, shaking his head— "I can't remember his name now."

"Wilson." His dad's voice was exact.

"Ah, of course. Wilson. Ok so, there was this boy. Boy named Wilson. And he was a big lump." He stretched the word *big* as his palms rose high, tracing the invisible lines of a broad-shouldered dome in the air. "A bloody huge lad."

"Pftt. Fat bloater," muttered his dad.

"And Wilson, well, I don't think he was a very happy person, to be honest, because—"

"He certainly wasn't in the end, was he." His dad's voice was strained, spoken through gritted teeth.

"Come on now, Arthur, I'm telling the story here. So, this boy Wilson, he couldn't have been a happy lad, because he was always trying to make other people unhappy. Shoving us other boys round—all of who were smaller than him, in our year, at least—and calling us nasty names, threatening to thump you if you didn't give him this chocolate, that pencil, or your lunch money and so on. He used to tease your dad about his acne, something rotten. Your dad hadn't done anything to Wilson, but he called him horrible, hurtful names, all the same. Was right out of order. Was horrible. And, more than a few times, Wilson did thump other boys. They ended up with eyes as blue as that t-shirt you got on. Or bloody noses, or sore guts if he hit them there. He was a right bruiser, was Wilson. He did boxing, you see. And bloody hell, did he have a wallop on him. Even at his age. Nobody else could—"

"Were you scared of him?" Jack knew Hendy

didn't get angry at interrupting questions when he told stories. In fact, he seemed to like it.

He pursed his lips and took a quick sip. "That's a very good question, actually. Hmm was I scared of him? Well, I was, and I wasn't."

"What do you mean?" Either he was or he wasn't, in Jack's mind. You couldn't be both.

"Well, I was scared of fighting him one to one, because I wouldn't have had a bloody chance. And, as well as getting bashed black and blue, my old man would have seen me with black eyes or bruises, whatever, and he would have given me a hiding too, for fighting at school. No doubt about that. So that was a losing situation. But"—he tapped his temple twice— "something inside me always knew that anyone made of flesh and bone can't be completely feared all the time. Cause they're just same as you and me; they're not made of bloody titanium, are they? For example, I knew that if a boy like Wilson"— he shrugged, waving his free palm casually— "were to say...have an accident, he'd get hurt just like anyone else, wouldn't he?"

"But most people don't have accidents at school?"

Hendy gave a nod of agreement. "You're right about that, Jack. Most people aren't that unlucky, are they? And in your schools nowadays, it's all health and safety, isn't it? Be careful of this, watch out for that, try not to put your teacher up the duff—"

"Ha!" His dad interrupted with the crack of a sharp laugh.

Smiling broadly, Hendy continued. "But it wasn't like that back then. Nobody gave a monkey's about safety when me and your dad were kids. Ain't that right, Arthur?"

"Absolutely. Schools were dangerous places, back then," he said, stroking his moustache and smirking. "Well go on then, Rudyard bloody Kipling. Get on with your story. I want to hear the good bit."

Hendy sat up and leaned forward towards Jack. "See, our school was an old Victorian building. Stone steps and shaky old iron handrails. And those steps had seen a lot of footfall; a lot of shoes rubbing them smooth over the decades. Made them slippery. The library ones were the worst. Two long flights of steep steps separated by a stone landing. You had to be careful on those steps"—he tipped a mouthful of beer— "especially on the way down. And well, wouldn't you know it? One day, poor Wilson, he had an accident down those steps."

"What happened?"

"Well, one hour a day you had library time. You were supposed to read for fun—Read for fun? Yea, that was funny in itself—and Wilson usually went to the toilet at least twice during that hour. Probably all the lemonade and juice he was taking from other boys, made him need to go so much. He was probably in such a hurry to relieve himself that he forgot how smooth the steps were and slipped. And oh Christ"—Hendy shook his square head— "he took a nasty tumble, didn't he, Arthur?"

"Very nasty," his dad said, with a flutter of eyebrows and thin grin.

"But the funny thing was, when he got up from falling down the first set of steps, all dazed, delirious, and believe me, his face was covered in blood from smashing his nose—or must have been, should I say—he went stumbling around and the silly bugger only fell down the next set of steps too. All the way down. Was lucky he didn't break his bloody neck, to be honest."

"Yea, that would have been tragic. Bloody tragic." His dad's smile was the broadest it had been in months. Jack always felt most on edge when his dad looked happy.

But he needed to know. "So, what happened to Wilson, in the end? Was he ok?"

"Well,"—Hendy bunched his cheek to the side, making a wet clicking sound— "he smacked his head so many times off that stone, smacked it so hard. He was never the same again. He stayed on at our school—coming back after about four months in hospital—but after he came back, he talked funny, walked funny"—Hendy stuck his tongue out, screwed up his face and shook his body— "like that. Injury to the brain, so we heard. Struggled at everything after that."

Teeth softly resting on his lower lip, his dad

eased them off, opened his mouth and the words oozed as he said with a smug smile, "Especially fighting."

CHAPTER 5

The vehicle waiting to pick them up was bigger than the train station they'd arrived at. It looked like three big cars joined together; like a long, chunky gemstone polished to perfection, sat upon four silver coins glistening in the Scottish sun. Jack was in awe.

Hendy let out a whisp of a whistle as he ran his eyes along its shiny black surface. "Nice. Nice motor. That's a stretch limo, Jack. A bloody huge one too."

Behind them, beside the platform where they'd got off the train, stood the station's red brick shack with its rust-speckled sign saying Auchtercluchty. And that was it. Nothing else. They were surrounded by waves of hills; their emerald meadows dotted with sheep and divided by short stone walls. It was so peaceful, the silence complete, save for occasional gentle bleats from passing sheep.

The blue sky's breeze was wafting through his hair, blowing cool kisses against his head. Jack filled his lungs with fresh air. He was glad to have a change of location. The train compartment had started to feel cramped after so many hours stuck in it with his dad.

Standing beside the limo was its driver. He was dressed in a smart navy suit, white shirt and red tie which puffed out sideways, like a bow on a present. And he was wearing a turban. Jack knew that because one of the teachers at school was Indian and wore the same thing. It was wrapped round his head like luxuriant blue rose petals, secured in the middle with a pin.

As they walked down the steps towards the car, Jack's dad muttered to Hendy, "We getting a VIP trip to a curry house or what." Both sniggering, they stepped towards the driver with Jack following behind.

"Is one of you gentlemen Mr Ravensthorpe?"

"Yea, that's me," replied his dad.

"Excellent, sir. Good evening to all of you fine gentlemen. I trust you had a pleasant journey. My name is Harbir, and I will be driving you to Mr De Luca's estate. The limousine is stocked with refreshments, so please help yourselves. The drive will take approximately one hour." His tone was humble, friendly. Jack guessed he was a good driver.

"Thank you very much, Harbir. Pleasure to meet you," said Hendy, flashing his black and gold grin.

"Same here," said his dad with a slight nod.

"Hi, Harbir," said Jack, which earned him a wink and hello in reply.

Their bags stored in the enormous boot, they were nestled in luxury leather and on their way further into the highlands. The inside was smaller than their living room, but much nicer. Everything was new, spotless. Jack could smell lime or lemon in the air. Seating stretched down one side in a black and white leather sofa and across from that was a big TV set into the wall. It sat above gleaming shelves with fancy long glasses hanging in special holders—to stop them falling over when the car was moving—and underneath that was a leather-topped counter with baskets of fruit, crisps, chocolates and pastries. Below that were four glass-doored fridges full of cans and bottles.

Jack caressed the leather seat with his palm. It was smooth and soft. He stretched out. So much room for a car. "It smells like fresh lemons in here," he said to Hendy, who was sitting next to him.

Hendy reached forward towards the fridges and pulled out a fancy bottle with a white label and puffy top coated in gold foil, which he peeled off, unwinding the mesh wiring over its bulbous cork.

"Nah"—the cork fired into the ceiling with a loud pop, giving Jack a fright — "it smells like money."

Jack chose a cola and crisps while Hendy poured fizzy wine into two glinting glasses. Its froth spilled over the sides, dripping onto the ridged rubber flooring. His dad sipped; Hendy guzzled.

"Don't go drinking too much and getting mouthy with people, ok? I mean it," his dad said to Hendy.

Hendy nodded at the bubbling pale liquid in the glass—its fragrance was crisp, like dried pears served on even drier biscuits— "Take a couple of gallons of this grape juice to have me even half-cut. Relax, Arthur."

"Just don't go on nothing stronger than wine. And take it easy. We're not here for a knees up. I'm clear on that, aren't I?"

Hendy nodded before reaching forward and taking a large, iced pastry from one of the baskets, ripping it in half and chomping. It lasted about ten seconds between his bulldog jaws.

With an electric hum, the screen between their lounge and the driver's area came down until they could see the back of Harbir's turban as he steadied the steering wheel with subtle turns. He was wearing tight tan leather gloves secured on his wrists with shiny black buttons. Jack wondered if everyone who worked for Dante De Luca dressed so elegantly.

"So, gentlemen, first time in Scotland?" asked Harbir with a flash of eyes in the rear-view mirror.

"Been to Edinburgh before. Long time ago. Walked round the castle and that. How about you, where you from?" asked his dad before knocking back the wine. He planted the empty glass on the leather counter with a soft thud.

"Originally from Punjab in India, sir, but I've been here in Mr De Luca's service for more than ten years now."

"Punjab, eh? Bit far from home ain't ya? How'd you meet Mr De Luca then?"

They were driving alongside a lake now. Jack turned in the leather seat, leaning his arm on its top. He looked through shaded glass to admire the meeting of water and land. Lined with flourishing grass, and trees heavy with healthy leaves, the lake's surface was rippling from breeze. Would have made a lovely drawing.

"It's a long story, sir. Suffice to say, I was of help to him when he made a sale to one of the princes in Punjab. He kindly offered me employment soon after."

"Prince, eh? Has some fancy customers, doesn't he?"

"That he does, sir." Jack noticed Harbir's eyes searching for him in the mirror. "And you must be Jack, am I correct?"

"Yes, sir," replied Jack, using his jeans to rub salt and crisp crumb from his fingers.

"You must have quite a talent, Jack. Mr De Luca has been incredibly fussy in his search for an apprentice. Even to make it to the test says remarkable things about you."

"Fussy? Thirty odd years and never picked one. I should say so," said Hendy before crinkling open a crisp bag.

His dad's lips formed a wry grin. "Has to happen sooner or later doesn't it?"

The limo wound its way between mountains and past more lakes. Jack's curiosity was surging. Alongside his anxiety.

❊ ❊ ❊

"I'm sorry sir, no photos," said Harbir with a firm tone and broad smile.

"What?"

Jack could hear the tension in his dad's tongue as it flicked the fast question. He didn't like being told no.

"Yes"—Harbir shrugged— "I'm afraid Mr De Luca is a very private person. He doesn't allow photography anywhere on the grounds. In fact, all guests must deposit their phones—and any cameras they have—in the safe on arrival. Returnable upon departure, of course."

They had arrived at Dante De Luca's house. It was nothing like Jack had imagined. He thought only kings and queens lived in palaces.

As soon as the limo had stopped in front, both his dad and Hendy had opened the sliding door and pulled out their phones, marvelling, keen to take pictures. Grey gravel crunched under their feet. This stuff was laid thick though, and no patches. Not like the driveway at Jack's house.

He counted five floors. Not high compared to London skyscrapers, but the ornate stonework and glimmering windows stretched so far in each direction, he was struggling to see the corners. The front entrance area jutted from the main building. It was a triangular-roofed block braced by five huge columns. In the space between the roof and the top of the columns was a picture story carved in stone, like old Greek buildings he'd seen on TV. There was a giant creature. Its head and wings were like an eagle, but the body looked more like a big cat. Jack guessed a lion, as there were no stripes or spots chiselled onto its muscular frame. In any case, it was facing off against six wolves, the largest of which was being crunched in its enormous beak. He wondered if Dante De Luca had sculpted that himself.

Harbir was popping the boot as he spoke, pulling the straps of all their bags over one shoulder with no sign of strain. He was stronger than he looked.

"I'm not sure I'm happy putting my phone in your safe," said his dad, putting it back in his pocket. "What if I have to make an emergency call?"

"Every guest room has a landline, you may call wherever you like for as long as you like, free of charge. Even internationally if needed."

"And what if someone needs to get hold of me?"

"Well, sir"—he shifted the bag straps further, close to his neck— "I'm afraid the rules are the rules. One thing I can say though is, this is an opportunity of a lifetime for your son. You don't want to damage it for the sake of a brief time without your phone, I'm sure. Now, if you would like to follow me to the reception."

Both tutting and mumbling, his dad and Hendy made no offer to help carry the bags.

Their mood seemed to improve in the reception hall. The smiling woman holding a clipboard was much taller than either of them. Shiny blonde hair in a bun with eyes blue as the summer sky, she looked like a Viking. A pretty girl one, of course, not the scary men with big beards and axes. Hendy's eyes were fixed on the large bumps under her tight white blouse as he said, "Evening, miss. And how are you today?" His voice was different, more delicate. Like he was hopeful she'd give him money or something.

Why did men care so much about women's chests? They were interesting, sure, but only for a few seconds. Staring at them constantly didn't give any benefit except sore eyes. Both Hendy and his dad were talking to her upper body more than her face. That seemed quite rude to Jack.

They discussed rooms and handed her their phones amidst grins, chuckles and jokes Jack thought were silly. She smiled too, but in short, business-like bursts, like a school headmistress. Her English was better than most English people's, but the accent didn't sound like a UK one.

He looked at the floor. It was made of large black and white marble squares, like a chessboard. The wooden doors they'd walked through had chunky brass handles and a huge keyhole on one side. He could smell something nice like vanilla and roses. Probably furniture polish because there weren't any real flowers in the reception hall. On the opposite side were another two large doors with six glass panels in each. Peering through, he saw the hall beyond. It looked long as a town high street.

The tall lady was pointing to places in a framed floor plan on the wall. "Here, in the banquet hall, there is a buffet being served for arriving guests. You are also welcome to relax and mingle with the other guests here and here in the adjoining drawing room and cigar lounge. The south terrace can be accessed from here. Ronald here will show you to your rooms"—she gestured to a redheaded man in a black waistcoat and tie — "and please feel free to ask for anything you need."

"Alright, thank you very much"—his dad took the three rooms sets of jingling keys from her outstretched palm, giving one to Hendy— "and when will we be meeting Mr De Luca?"

"The painting test begins tomorrow at noon. He'll be introducing himself then."

"Not tonight? I was hoping to have a word with him before the start of the, uh, test."

"I'm afraid that's impossible, Mr Ravensthorpe. He's deeply immersed in one of his paintings just now and can't be disturbed."

Painting test? Jack had thought he'd be allowed to do a drawing for Dante De Luca. He didn't know a thing about painting. He hoped at least some of the other apprentice hopefuls were as clueless as him. Otherwise, he was going to look stupid. And that would make his dad upset.

Ronald—who seemed Scottish from the way he talked—loaded their bags onto a fancy trolley with a red felt base and gleaming brass frame. They followed him as he pushed it down a wide corridor with walls panelled in walnut-coloured wood. High over their heads hung lights made of crystals bunched together, hanging in sparkling strips. They were chandeliers, his dad said. Ronald ushered them into a lift walled with mirrors and silver railings.

After getting out of the lift on the 4th floor, they were still walking through the corridors five minutes later. Jack noticed there were no paintings on the walls. Wouldn't such a famous painter want his work hanging everywhere? Jack would have.

"Mr De Luca should invest in some golf carts. How big is this place for Christ's sake?" asked his dad.

"Aye, it is a fair stroll to your rooms right enough sir, but I think you'll be pleasantly surprised at the accommodations. Well worth the walk, I assure you," replied Ronald in a melodious lilt, like birds chirping over the trolley's grumbling trundle.

CHAPTER 6

Ronald was right. It was awesome. Like having his own dream room for a night.

The first thing Jack noticed was the bed in the centre. It was three times the size of his one at home. Covered in flawless white sheets and six puffy pillows, it looked like a square of solid cotton ointment for his tired body and aching feet.

He slipped his trainers off and slid onto its surface, squeezing one of the pillows in a cuddle. It was the perfect balance of solid and squidgy.

Wrapping himself round it tighter, he lay his head on the one underneath and took in what was around him. It was incredible. Like the fanciest hotel in the world. Had his drawing really been *that* good to deserve this treatment?

Uncurling himself from the bed, he sat with his feet pressed on thick carpet. Taking off his socks, he rubbed bare soles on soft, welcoming fibres. The gentle friction sent rubs of relaxation all the way from toe to tummy.

And what a TV; like a door turned lengthways. Underneath it was—oh my. The latest games console everyone was talking about. What surprised him was, he didn't think it was even in shops yet. Not only that, but beside it was piled a stack of games, their rectangular cases all coated in unbroken cellophane. He hadn't played video games in years. His dad said they were a waste of money. Maybe this special occasion called for a treat?

Jack opened the fridge in the corner to find every kind of fizzy drink imaginable. Two of each type. He chose his favourite cola and plunged the can open with a hiss, releasing sweet smoke. The fizzles met his tongue and throat with frosty washes as he guzzled, gasping in pleasure at the biting refreshment. Wonderful.

The wide window was tall as a basketball player and framed between red velvet curtains; they were tied with golden ropes secured by hooks the same colour. Beneath its sill stood a shining brown desk. It had two documents laid on its centre: one was a leatherbound booklet—it said 'Room Service Menu'—and the other an envelope. His name was elegantly written on the top in rich black ink.

Beside it was a silver sliver, around four inches long, with sides and top a little sharper than a breadknife. His dad had a similar tool back at home. It was for opening letters. His dad's one was shaped like a sword. The one Jack now held was a mini paintbrush.

Nestling it between the top folds, he drew the slender brush across, enjoying the satisfying sight and sound of the envelope's straight tear. The cream paper inside—thick and rigid between his fingers—held a message written in equal elegance and shade. It read like this:

Dear Jack,

Welcome to my home. I was impressed by your drawing. It is an honour to have you as my guest. Tomorrow is your day to shine. Sleep well, and do not trouble yourself with thoughts of failure or success, because success only follows repeated experiences of failure. The two are intertwined, always. Try your best and believe in yourself.
See you tomorrow at noon.

Warmest regards,

Dante De Luca

Wow. So that was from Dante De Luca himself. It was kind of him to write Jack a note personally. He was still worried about the test though. He had no clue how to paint well. But he would take Mr De Luca's advice: Try his best and believe in himself.

Food would help distract him from nerves. He opened the menu. He'd never had room service before. And he might never again.

Running his eyes down the lists of meals, he noticed it was all things that boys his age would like. There were no fancy dishes whose names he didn't recognize. Fish and chips, burgers, pies, sausages, spaghetti; he could have whatever he wanted, delivered right to his room, like he was royalty or something. All he had to do was dial zero on the bedside phone. But what was he going to eat? There were so many choices, and he was ravenous. He sipped at the cola as he tried to decide.

Then his dad opened the door. Jack put the menu down and sat on the edge of the bed, can in hand. Before coming into the room, his dad spoke to Hendy, saying, "I'll be down in a bit. And bloody behave yourself, all right?"

His dad had taken off his jacket and tie and changed the white shirt to a light blue one. The sleeves were rolled to his elbows. His forearms weren't as huge as Hendy's, but they still looked hard as hammers. The veins ran plentiful and blue, criss-crossing twitching muscles. Jack got a flash of the wound on his palm. It was thick, pink, like half-cooked meat.

There were two black leather armchairs on circular stands in front of the TV. He swivelled one to face Jack and sat in it. Rubbing his hands along its puffy arms, he said, "This is nice"—he gestured round the room with his eyes— "all of this, I mean. Isn't it?"

He hesitated before answering. "Yes, dad. Really nice. Thank you for bringing me."

Shifting in the chair, he tutted and shook his head softly. "No, Jack. Thank *you*. Without your artistic skills, we wouldn't be here. Now"— he ran his tongue along his lower lip then shifted again— "you in it to win it?"

He wanted to promise his dad he'd be the first winner ever, but it felt like a lie. And what good came of lies?

"I've never painted before, dad, but I promise I'll do my best."

Eyelids narrowing, his dad smiled in a way that spoke the opposite. He ran fingertips from the centre of his moustache, outwards in both directions. Perching forward in the chair, stare accompanied by scowl, he was causing Jack's neck to tremble. There was silence, except for tiny tinkles of fizz tapping the inside of the cola can in Jack's hand.

"Oh, I see. Your best. Ok." Tone whispered, he stopped stroking his moustache before saying, "You see, son, losers always talk about doing their best. Cause that's all they can do, right? Their so-called best. Whereas winners"—palms spread outwards, he looked round the room before focusing again on Jack— "winners get stuff like this. And I want some of this. Getting thirty grand for staying in a palace, well that's sweet. I thought that was a stroke of luck. Easy money, after all. But now? Now I've seen all this? Let's just say my whistle's been wetted. You learn to paint like this De Luca fella and just imagine. No more worries for you or your poor old dad ever again. No more worries about money, about nothing."

He stood, walking over to caress Jack's cheek; the rough skin of the cut along his palm scraping in a way that had Jack wanting to fidget free. "No more worries, all thanks to you, Little Picasso. I know you won't let me down."

Removing his hand, he nodded to the door. "You coming down to eat? Mingle, see the other kids?"

"I thought—"

"Yea, I thought as much. That's ok though. You relax, rest, get a good sleep. Save all your vitals for tomorrow."

His dad left, closing the door behind him with a gentle click.

Jack looked at the room service menu. He'd lost his appetite.

CHAPTER 7

Jack was in an amphitheatre. That was what the Viking lady had called it as she'd escorted all the hopefuls and their parents into the brightly lit hall. A half-circle of shiny red leather seats in rows, all fixed on a giant platform of stepped white marble; Jack thought it was a bit like a cinema, but old-fashioned. There was no screen to watch a movie.

There was him instead. Along with six other boys and girls who were sitting in the central space, staring at blank canvases rested on broad black easels, with sets of paintbrushes, pallets and—of course—paint arranged on wooden trolleys beside them. Four boys and two girls; the youngest looked at least three years older than him and the oldest was near to university age. They all had one thing in common though, and that was clear eagerness.

Jack was envious. A part of him wished he'd never taken an interest in art. It would have been safer to fail at football or rugby. Mediocrity in maths or chess might not have landed him where he was now: at the centre of his dad's grand expectations.

The creaky, three-legged stool he sat on wasn't in line with the luxury of the palace. After only ten minutes perched on its solid surface, aches were nagging his backside. Shifting, he searched for a comfortable position but found none. He wanted to ask for a cushion, but nobody else had and he didn't want to be the first. Maybe putting up with discomfort was another part of the test?

At the side of the hall, double doors opened. Nobody entered. He looked into the rows to see the parents in the viewing area craning, peering, staring; pairs of mums and dads accompanied everyone, except him. He saw his dad focused on the doorway too, eyelids slitted, hunched forward. Hendy was the only one not frozen in anticipation. Leaning back into leather, he winked at Jack with a toothy, golden grin and flicked a chunky thumb upwards.

And in strode a man. If he was Dante De Luca, he wasn't what Jack had been expecting. Didn't rich people wear fancy clothes? This guy looked like he'd spent the night on a bench in Hyde Park. Almost, anyway. He was wearing a sweater, jeans and shoes, all plain black.

They were splashed and sprayed in streaks and patches of pastel and dark shades, a riot of chaotic colour, mingled with brilliant white and mottled grey. Jack got the feeling it wasn't a fashion statement.

The most unusual thing though, was his hairstyle. Like a sheep was trying out the Mohican look. Grey puffy tufts in a—sort of—triangle, pointed to the sky. He would have been two or three inches shorter than Jack's dad, if not for the hair. Marbled in thick black and white curls, his beard was a bush you could lose a golf ball in.

Everyone else in the palace was so perfect in their dress and grooming, but this was their boss? Really? Maybe he wasn't Dante De Luca?

"I am Dante De Luca." The voice was confident, clear and buzzing with vibrance as he addressed everyone in the hall. The rows were alive with wide eyes and whispered surprise. "Welcome to my home, and"—he faced the candidates — "a special welcome to all of you. It takes great courage to open one's passion to scrutiny. I salute you all." He did a half bow and stood straight again. "And now"—he signalled with two crisp claps— "the subject matter." A butler in black waistcoat and tie appeared through the doors, carrying a lumpy object draped in a white silk scarf. Handing it to Dante De Luca, he did a quick head bow, turned and left.

There was a small stage in front of the painting area with a square wooden table placed in the middle. Nothing else. Nothing on the table and nothing around it.

Climbing three steps, their host stood beside the table. Still holding the scarf-covered item, he looked across the amphitheatre and then at Jack and the other contestants. His eyes were searching, dazzling; he seemed to look at nobody but also at everybody, individually. His gaze met Jack's, and he was sure the tops of those bearded cheeks crinkled a fraction in affection, only for a millisecond. Or had they?

"For almost forty years I have searched for an apprentice. And in all that time I have seen so many talented individuals. So many young people sure to make their own special mark on the world of art, forging new paths with brushes dripping in brilliance. Believe me when I say you are all special and capable of remarkable things. Therefore, I also say to you brave souls who have come to prove your worth today: do not let my own unique"—he paused and smiled— "criteria discourage you from following your dreams. Should you not be chosen, it is not a reflection upon your abilities, but merely my preferences, which are extremely specific."

Commanding, captivating, his voice pierced the silence which had blanketed the hall. It echoed over leather, bounced off walls and battered from floor to ceiling; powerful, driven and demanding attention. Jack's focus was channelled, no longer mindful of the wild hair and shabby, paint spattered clothing.

"But who knows? Perhaps today will finally be the day? I certainly hope so, sincerely. To provide the answer one way or another, we have our subject matter"—he nodded to what was in his hands— "a simple but effective item to test your capabilities without fuss."

Placing the object on top of the table with a light clunk, he withdrew its veil of silk secrecy.

It was a large bowl of fruit: bananas, strawberries, green apples, oranges and red grapes.

"Parents, please observe the candidates only and do not talk to them. Candidates, please complete your work in silence unless I—and only I—speak to you. If you need something, please raise your hand. The time limit is four hours"—he pointed to a large clock on the wall above him—"so please feel free to start. You may paint in any style you wish. Now is your time to shine. Power to your paintbrushes!"

Jack glanced round the hall at his competitors. They were already getting to work, examining brushes, squeezing paint from silver tubes or coloured bottles, mixing on their palettes and scrutinizing the fruit bowl with pursed lips and eyes brimming with purpose.

He looked at his own equipment. He hadn't a clue. All he could do was try his best.

THE PAINTER'S APPRENTICE

※ ※ ※

Jack's brush bristles were teasing the canvas in timid smudges, forming the semblance of a banana. It looked like a banana to him, anyway. He'd squeezed yellow paint from one of the tubes and spread it across a small section of the palette's edge. Then he'd done the same with black, because he was trying to define the sides of the fruit with fine lines. Looked better than he'd expected.

That wasn't saying much. He didn't dare look at what the other kids were doing. Focusing on his canvas only, all he could hear was their hushed speech across the silent hall as Dante De Luca asked them questions about their paintings. One girl had mentioned "tackling fruit with the surrealist approach," to which their judge had replied, "Yes, and you succeed. It speaks of Dali." And then another boy—probably the oldest looking one, from the depth of his posh voice—talked with intimidating certainty on "the simplicity of a watercolour in the manner of the great Monet." The reply given was, "Yes, yes, I see. An ambitious and bold feat indeed." Another of the boys had spoken enthusiastically about "an attempt to bridge impressionism and cubism, with Cezanne in mind," to the tune of "Bravo, young man."

These conversations—the confidence and complicated references further convincing Jack he had no business being there—continued until the man himself stood next to him. Odours of tobacco and paint fumes wisped as the judge crouched, smiling in reassurance. Bushy whiskers bobbing, he said, "So, tell me about your work."

"Erm, well"—Jack searched for something clever to say, like the other kids had— "I erm...I've finished two of the bananas."

He broke into a chuckle. "Indeed, you"—he peered at the canvas, eyelids narrowing at first, then peeling right back, his eyes bulging, wild— "indeed you—"

Standing with a stagger, he used Jack's shoulder to steady himself, putting all his weight on it. Jack was glad Mr De Luca wasn't Hendy's size or he would have been knocked off the stool. His chest rising and falling rapidly; the wrinkled caramel skin of his face had turned a shade paler.

"Are you ok, Mr De Luca?" His painting wasn't *that* bad, was it?

With a quivering smile he steadied on his feet, breathing hard through circled lips. Jack heard shoes clacking over the marble and looked across to see a butler hurrying towards them with a face frowning in concern. Mr De Luca held up his palm as signal to stop, and then waved him away. Everyone was looking now.

His voice was tinged with tremble when he asked, "You must be Jack, the sketcher, yes? You've never painted before, I assume?"

"No, sir." That wasn't like the questions he'd asked the others. He looked at his painting, and then at Mr De Luca, who was disturbed, staring at those bananas like they were fruity ghouls dancing around the canvas. He heard a stifled giggle from one of the nearby girls. His work was a big joke.

Not a funny one though. And he could feel his dad's eyes burning into him from the rows above. The journey back to London was going to be bad.

CHAPTER 8

The final minute of the fourth hour had expired. The competition was over. All the paintings were lined up beside each other.

Six works of wonder rested on easels. And Jack's. He felt embarrassed. The other contestants' work looked professional; his was like primary school class gone wrong.

Looking into the rows, he saw parents, proud, smiling, hopeful, as Mr De Luca inspected the canvases. But not his dad. There was no pride. No smile. And he didn't look hopeful.

The contestants were now sitting in the front seats of the amphitheatre. Jack's painting was last in the display, and he was sat furthest from everyone, near the corner. Feeling glad of leather cushioning instead of the solid wooden stool, he eased into it but still couldn't relax. The discomfort had moved from his bum to his brain.

Mr De Luca inspected the competition entries with a stroll and a smile. He stopped at the end and paused, staring at Jack's fruit bowl. Once again, the eyes flared in their sockets, before he looked at Jack with an unsettled expression.

It was the best fruit bowl he could have done. It was his very first. What could anyone expect? Picasso?

Walking to the corner where he was sitting, Mr De Luca turned and stood with his back to Jack before addressing the other contestants. "You should all be extremely proud of yourselves. Six works worthy of the Louvre itself have been created this afternoon. You are all young people of incredible talent and have bright futures ahead of you. Thank you so much, for the honour of witnessing your artistry in action. I salute you all. But, my friends, I regret I will not be choosing any of you as my apprentice."

Sighs and grumbles rumbled around the circular seating, from both the children and their parents. Dreams had been burst like balloons. At least they were getting told to their faces. And *Six* works. Not seven. *Six*. He was miffed.

The side doors opened again. Two butlers stood holding silver trays stacked with envelopes. The tall blonde lady was there too. "I understand your disappointment, but, as I said before, this is not a reflection on your abilities. You should take your paintings home and hang them with pride. I wish you all the best of luck in what are sure to be illustrious careers in painting. Now, if you could please exit from these doors"—he pointed towards the staff— "Miss Karlsson will ensure you are given the agreed payment for participation and travel expenses. There are limousines waiting to take you to the train station. Thank you and have a safe journey home."

Why had he been forced to stare at Dante De Luca's paint spattered back? That was plain rude. It was like Jack wasn't even included. He'd tried his best, like he'd been told, hadn't he?

The—no longer—hopefuls gathered their works and were filing through the doors, alongside their parents who were collecting envelopes as they passed. There was shuffle and scuff across marble as the hall emptied.

Slinking off the seat, Jack walked towards the doors, dejected, fearful of his dad's anger. He didn't even care about taking his painting. Head down, he walked past Dante De Luca, embarrassed—and a bit annoyed—not wanting to say goodbye.

"Not you."

He turned to see Dante De Luca standing with a sly smile, barely visible between his bushy curls.

"Sorry?"

"I said not you."

"But I—"

"Follow me." He turned to a door behind and opened it, walking through while saying, "Come on, Jack. I don't have all day."

So, he followed. Anything that would delay talking to his dad was welcome. Jack walked into what looked like a waiting room.

He was met by a giant. Tall as a tree and wide as a wardrobe, he was an African man with a shiny head like Hendy's. His massive arms folded, their muscles bulging under a thin black cotton sweater; he was standing in front of another door. It had a golden plaque on it which said Dante's Office.

Mr De Luca seemed hurried, excited. "Oh, Jack, this is Jaheem. Jaheem, this is Jack. Jack, please wait there while I arrange some things. Help yourself to drinks and snacks." He pointed to one of the two mahogany brown leather sofas. There was a glass-doored fridge full of cans and a table with biscuits, crisps and cakes. The enormous man moved to the side. Dante De Luca went into the office and closed the door behind with a hasty clunk.

What was going on? He fished into the fridge and cracked open his favourite cola. Whatever was happening, there was no point in having a dry throat.

"Do you want one?" he asked the massive guy.

"No thanks, Jack." The face was stony, but his voice was polite.

He was curious. "How—"

"Seven feet six inches."

"Wow that's really—"

The door swung open, and his dad and Hendy marched in. Their shoes scraped on the marble as they came to a sudden halt, both stiffening with surprise at the towering size of the man blocking the door to Dante De Luca's office.

Then Jack's dad turned to him, scowling. The clothes were still fancy, but his manner wasn't. Lumpy cheeks patched in pink, he said, "I might have known you'd be bloody useless. Do you know how embarrassing that was for me? Eh?"

"You should calm down," said Jaheem. His tone was flat, emotionless. Shoulders like bowling balls, they were far wider than the door he was guarding.

Craning his neck, Jack's dad spoke quickly, his head twitching, shaking. "Calm down? Calm down? I was promised thirty grand to come here. The bird at the other side didn't have no envelope for me, says no cheque's been written for me neither. Now"—he pointed at Jack with a backwards thumb while staring up at Jaheem— "I don't care how shit his painting was, I want the money I was promised. Is De Luca in there? I want a word."

"He's busy, you'll have to wait."

"I don't feel like waiting. I want a word right now."

"It's not my job to care what you want."

"You what?" His dad took a step closer, having to move his head back even further to keep eye contact.

"Come on now, Arthur. Give the big fella a break," said Hendy.

Waving his finger at Jaheem's face, he said, "That old duffer in there owes me thirty grand, and I want to talk to him about it. And you're in my way. One way or another, you're getting out of my way. We understand each other?"

Arms still crossed in sinewy folds; Jaheem stooped. Their faces were inches apart. "I understand that you need to calm down."

Jack saw Hendy slip his right hand into his jacket pocket, fumbling. He drew it out again, letting it hang slightly behind his hip. The knuckles of his fist were circled in thick metal rings all moulded together. Looked like copper? Or Brass? But, what? That was crazy. With Hendy's muscles, if he punched someone with that, it would be like a hammer!

"Arthur, look at the size of this lump. You've got some *brass* neck squaring up to him. Step back, me old China," said Hendy, patting his dad's back and grinning at Jaheem.

Nodding, his dad took a couple of steps backwards but wasn't finished speaking. "I'll slap you back to umba gumba land, or wherever the hell you're from." Taking off his tie and unbuttoning the top button of his shirt, he stood huffing, fists clenched and face scarlet.

Jaheem—now standing straight again—was staring down at Hendy; their heads separated by a considerable height difference. Both chuckling, smiling, but Jack got the feeling neither of them were sincere. Why did people smile when they didn't mean it?

The giant unfolded his arms, revealing a chest like slabs of granite. He said to Hendy, "You think you know me? You smile like a crocodile. Only with uglier teeth. Try it. I dare you. I'll take those knuckle dusters off you and shove them right up your ar—"

"Arthur Ravensthorpe?" Dante De Luca's head was poking out of the open office door, around the side of Jaheem. His voice was excited, friendly, as if he had no idea of the problem in the waiting room.

His dad stepped forward, "Now look here—"

"Mr Ravensthorpe! I am so sorry to keep you waiting. I was just preparing the contract."

"Contract? What contract?"

"For the apprenticeship, of course."

The metal rings disappeared back into Hendy's jacket pocket. Scowl on his dad's pink cheeks reformed into surprise. Jack dropped his cola on the floor.

CHAPTER 9

A grin spread across his dad's cheeks as Dante De Luca pulled the cheque from its stub with a crisp tear along its perforated edge. Sitting behind his chunky wooden desk—the top cluttered with papers, books and pots of pens—the painter of fame was no less scruffy, but his eccentric manner had swayed business-like.

"So, we are clear on the terms then, Mr Ravensthorpe?" His smile was soft, but the words clicked in sharp syllables.

"Oh absolutely, Mr De Luca. As crystal."

"Because I cannot stress enough the rigidity of the contract terms. Even any minor deviation from them will result in immediate termination of the agreement, and stringent legal action"—he fluttered the cheque held between his fingers—"to recover all sums paid to you."

His dad's nod was rapid, the smile unbroken. "Absolutely, Mr De Luca, not a problem. The terms of the contract are more than satisfactory."

Eight years. The apprenticeship was for eight years. That meant Jack would be a grown-up by the end of it. His dad would only be allowed to visit once a year, with an appointment made one month in advance. And no phone calls to the palace unless a literal life-or-death emergency was involved. Dante De Luca had insisted the apprenticeship needed to be "immersive and without distraction" for Jack to learn the mastery of painting. Mastery? All the other candidates had made masterpieces. He could barely paint a banana. Why him? It was all so confusing.

But it was welcome. No more bullies. No more stupid creative writing class or boring English. He'd be able to study art all day long. And he already felt drawn to his new mentor. Dante De Luca was unusual—putting it mildly—but Jack sensed waves of genuine warmth from his eyes and smile. Such a contrast from his dad's disinterested grunts or angry glares.

It was a new life. It was like a dream. He hoped nobody would wake him.

Standing, Dante De Luca leaned over the desk towards the armchair his dad was sitting in and presented the cheque. "There we are then, the payment for the first year. One million pounds sterling. The same amount to be paid annually on this date, by bank transfer, until the end of your son's apprenticeship. And I have added on to it, the thirty thousand pounds for attendance and expenses, as promised."

Jack's dad was acting scarily polite. "Thank you very much, sir," he said before leaning back into the squeaking leather and holding the cheque up high with both hands. In his whole life, Jack had never heard his dad call another man sir. Not even the police when they visited the house. In fact, he'd heard him call them every name except sir.

"Obviously, with these being such large sums, and Jack being so young, the funds need to be entrusted into your care, as his father. You can give them to him when you feel it's the right time. But, of course, great care should be taken when allowing young men access to such wealth, don't you think?"

The back of the cheque was pale yellow; his dad's eyes glinted like the paper was made of solid gold. It was trembling in his grasp. "Couldn't agree more, Mr De Luca. And uh, sincere apologies for the misunderstanding earlier, with your man, Jaheem," said his dad with eyes flitting between the cheque and Dante De Luca.

"Yea, an unfortunate misunderstanding, Mr De Luca. I'm extremely sorry for any offence caused," said Hendy; his chunky throat trying its best to croak out sentences in a posh voice.

"Oh, entirely my fault"—the back of his

hand flicked outwards in a dismissive gesture — "and neither of you were hospitalized, so all's well that ends well."

Jack saw Hendy's brow flash into a furrow, the muscles in his jaw stiffening. Then he broke into a chuckle, his gold teeth glinting under the chandelier. "Yea, that's the main thing, that nobody got hurt."

The office was surprisingly modest in size, considering it was part of such an enormous palace. It was about as big as Jack's classroom at school, except luxurious. The walls were panelled in polished wood, the floor covered in thick rug—which was spongy under Jack's trainers as their tips pressed it—and there was a counter in the corner with fancy glass bottles full of amber and crimson liquids. Stale fumes of spicy sweetness seemed to coat every surface. There was an ashtray heaped with crumpled cigar stubs on Mr De Luca's desk. Jack guessed they were the source of the powerful aromas.

With one final flick of his eyebrows, Jack's dad folded the cheque and slid it inside his jacket. "So, Mr De Luca, if you don't mind me asking, once he's finished his apprenticeship, will he be able to...do paintings anywhere near as good as yours?" he asked, clearing his throat and tipping a mouthful from the lemonade can on the coffee table beside him. He'd been offered stuff from the bottles in the corner but refused. Hendy hadn't. He was swirling light brown liquid in a glittering glass and taking regular sips.

Palms outward, Mr De Luca shrugged. "Perhaps"—he looked at Jack, giving a mischievous wink— "but perhaps far better. I believe Jack has incredible potential. We shall have to see."

Jack's dad looked at him, gesturing with his head. "Say thank you to Mr De Luca for all this kindness he's showing you. Mind your manners."

"Thank you, sir. I promise I'll try my best in everything you teach me."

Leaning forward, his dad ruffled Jack's hair with a rough palm. "That's my boy, Jack. See, Mr De Luca? Always tries his best. What more can anyone do than that, eh?"

"Uh, Mr De Luca." Hendy's gruff voice rose in a tone showing curiosity.

"Yes, Mr... It's Henderson, yes?"

"Call me, Hendy, please." Jack saw the skin around his dad's eyes tighten into crinkles as Hendy took a large slurp from his drink. "So, I hope you don't mind me asking, but erm"—he nodded towards Dante De Luca's arm— "what happened?"

Hendy was talking about the scarring under Mr De Luca's right sleeve. He'd rolled it up a little while signing the contracts. Jack had noticed too, but of course not said anything.

"I don't think that's anybody's business but his, is it?" His dad's tone was politeness poured through a barb-wired strainer.

"Oh no, it's perfectly alright. Here"—he

pulled up the sleeve of paint-dappled cloth— "be my guest. I am not ashamed of my scars, nor the wisdom that accompanies them."

The skin of his arm was mottled in dark red, the lines mashed into his flesh. Healed remains of an injury that must have been horrible at the time. He held it out so everyone could see clearly. "A tattoo only teeth can give."

"Dog?" asked Hendy.

"Of a sort. While walking alone in an isolated territory I was unfamiliar with, I was set upon by wolves. And this"—he ran his finger along the marks— "was from the alpha of the pack. A vicious beast indeed. His jaws delivered this jagged kiss. I was lucky to survive."

Jack couldn't help himself. "How did you escape?"

Dante De Luca leaned forward, his eyes sly and voice husky as he said, "That wolf had its head ripped clean off."

"You ripped a wolf's head off?" Jack's dad asked, sounding uncertain.

He sat back in the chair and raised his eyebrows, wagging his finger slowly. "I said it had its head ripped off. I did not say I did the ripping."

Hendy perched forward; eyes focused on the scars of Mr De Luca's arm. "So then how did you—"

"Let's just say a friend came to the rescue, shall we? The important thing is I am here, wiser albeit less pretty than before. And"—he pulled the sleeve down to his wrist— "it taught me a vital lesson for life. Do you know what that is, Jack?"

"Erm, not sure, sir."

He looked into Jack's eyes with a kind smile and said, "Always be prepared, for there are wolves everywhere."

CHAPTER 10

So that was it. He watched as the limousine rumbled down the grey gravel path towards the tall iron gates. They opened, and off it went into the distance. Taking his dad and Hendy away in its shiny black shell.

Jack stood beside Dante De Luca at the entrance to the palace. Lukewarm wind was nudging his puffy grey hair side to side in gentle sways. The sky wasn't dull, but only slivers of blue peeked between clouds round as balls of cotton wool. Beyond the gates were the Scottish Highlands in their rolling green glory; mountainous wonder coated in forests, fields and lochs.

And he felt overwhelmed. He was living in a palace now. As an apprentice to a famous painter. Because he'd done a crappy painting of a bowl of fruit. What was going on?

Dante De Luca turned to face him. "So, you have questions, yes?"

Jack nodded. "A lot, sir."

He placed a hand on Jack's shoulder. The touch was light. "Jack, enough with the sir, please. I'm not a kni—actually, I am a knight, in Italy, at least—but anyway, please no more sir, or Mr, ok? Dante is my name. Please call me that."

"Yes Mr—"

"Mmm?"

"Dante."

Dante's chuckle was rich in crinkled cheek and low in flashy teeth. Genuine kindness glowed from his gaze. Jack didn't feel afraid of saying the wrong thing. It would take time to adjust.

"Hungry?"

"Not really, si—Dante."

"Ok. Later then. So"—he crouched, his eyes glinting— "want to see something cool?"

"Sure, I'd love to."

Standing, he stroked his bushy grey and black beard. "Do young people still use that word? Or is saying 'cool' in fact now uncool? You know these things, Jack. Help me out."

"Yea, cool is still cool." He found himself smiling.

"Cool is always cool, eh?"

"Yea, think so...Dante." Then they were both laughing. He loved Dante's soft, flowing words. The accent—Jack supposed it had to be

Italian—was delicate, different from the harsh voices at school and home.

"Walk with me, please Jack." They crunched on the path for a minute, until Dante turned and pointed to the palace. "What do you think? Pretty cool eh?"

"Yea, definitely. So cool."

Dante shrugged, the paint patches on his grubby sweater were a mixture of freshly stuck and flaking off. "I must be used to it. Come, dear apprentice. Let me show you my idea of what is *really* cool."

❋ ❋ ❋

"Dante?" Jack asked as they strolled over marble, past gleaming brass and polished wood. He liked the bright corridors with their soaring ceilings and sparkling chandeliers. Unlike his dad, Dante walked at a relaxed pace that Jack could easily keep up with.

"Yes, dear boy. Ask. Never be afraid to ask. We learn by asking questions and listening carefully."

"Why did you pick me? My painting was rubbish."

The corridor stretched in a straight line, the length of a football pitch. Dante kept walking, not looking across. "Is that so? And why was it rubbish?"

"Well, the other painters. Their paintings were brilliant."

He gave a quick nod. "Yes. Extraordinarily talented young people. I was impressed. I wish them well and"—his face turned towards Jack's as they continued walking— "they did not have your gift. That is why your painting was not rubbish."

"My gift? What gift? I only painted a bowl of fruit."

"No, you painted a bowl of food."

"But fruit is food. Everyone painted food?"

"Everyone brushed paint onto a canvas in artful strokes until the depiction of food was presented in a pleasant way. You painted food. That was why I almost had a heart attack when I saw your work."

"Oh, I hope you're feeling better now?" He was still confused.

Smiling, he brushed a delicate palm over Jack's crown. "After all these years, my search is over. I've never felt better."

At the end of the corridor was a huge set of chunky metal doors. The tough-looking texture of their surface suggested to Jack they were extremely strong. There were two uniformed men sitting guarding them: one at a desk and the other on a chair on the opposite side of the corridor. They caused Jack alarm, despite their friendly smiles.

They had machine guns. Black, sleek and with thin banana-shaped magazines poking from the bottoms, Jack had only seen guns like that—in fact, any real guns—at the airport. On their hips in holsters were pistols. They looked like the ones in cowboy films, only much bigger. The men were also wearing hard black vests, joined at the sides in thick velcro straps. The kind you wore to stop a bullet.

"Weapons are a necessary evil, Jack. Not my desire, but it is a dangerous world and what lies beyond these doors is of immeasurable value."

"Your paintings?"

"Yes. And before you know it, yours will hang beside mine."

Dante introduced Jack to the two security guards, then his thumb print and eye scan unlocked the doors with internal whirrs and clunks.

❈ ❈ ❈

After walking through the doors, which were

about a foot thick, they stood at the start of a tunnel. It was wide as a city street. The flooring formed in small circles of non-slip rubber, it extended down in a mild slope. Into darkness.

Dante took a step forward, but Jack hesitated. "Erm, it looks really dark down there."

"You are afraid of the dark?"

"Yes, sorry."

"Why be sorry? It just means you're clever. The darkness can sometimes hold danger. There might be something waiting to eat you, or, much more likely, you will walk into a door and bang your head. Don't be sorry for being clever, ok Jack?"

"Thanks, Dante. I'll try. Are there more light switches down there?" He pointed to the switch for the light they were standing under. The fancy glass of chandeliers had been replaced by bright neon.

Dante shook his head and loosed a light tut. "No need. We will walk, and the path will illuminate before us."

And so, they did. With each few steps they took down the tunnel, another light strip above would flicker and buzz alive, bathing their path in brightness.

"How's the light going on and we're not switching it?" asked Jack as they continued their casual stroll.

Dante looked at him with a stony face and said, "It's magic, Jack. Magical powers."

"What? Really? You must be joking?"

His eyes narrowed, the look simmering with seriousness. "You don't believe in magic?"

"Well, I suppose it's—"

Dante's lips sputtered chuckles, his chest shaking in wheezy laughter. "Automated lighting. Laser sensors. But technology is a kind of magic, no?"

They were both laughing as they reached the tunnel's end. He felt like he was going into a superhero's secret hideout. This was true adventure.

Another eye and thumb scan led more massive doors to open. They stepped through and—like the tunnel—crackle and buzz above saw the entire room light up.

But the word room was nowhere near enough to describe the area they stood in. Jack's jaws slackened in astonishment. It was a tremendous cavern. Bigger than any museum he'd ever seen.

"Holy crap!" Jack didn't like bad language—he'd promised himself he wouldn't talk like his dad—but the words popped out under pressure.

"Ha, told you it was cool, eh?"

"Wha—what is this place?"

"The most valuable collection of paintings in the entire world. I call it the Gallery of Galleries."

Jack felt like a hamster admiring a house. The place was a cathedral dedicated to Dante

De Luca's genius, with its walls trumpeting his praise through a chorus of unbelievable artistry. Every type of subject matter was on display; all blessed with eternity through masterful brushstrokes and housed in ornate golden rectangles. And not only the walls. The ceiling was also sublime. Squares and rectangles sang a symphony of breath-taking brilliance from above. Paintings, even up there? Incredible.

"This place is beyond cool. It's amazing," said Jack as he and Dante strolled over gleaming varnished wood. Smiling, Dante nodded without answer. There was silence, save for their footsteps and a slight hum from the lighting. Jack got the feeling he was being given a chance to revel in the moment.

The wonderful works were a variety of lengths and widths, but they tended towards large. Most were huge. The height of one man at a bare minimum. He didn't see any piddly ones like his bowl of fruit. And he noticed something peculiar.

They were all connected to a railing system; a network of sturdy black metal tracks running between and underneath each painting. "The tracks?"

"I have so many—"

"How many are there? Oh, sorry." Excitement was melting manners.

"It's ok"—he gave Jack's head a soft pat — "I'm not your father, Jack. I'm not here to scold you for enthusiasm. And there are"—he squinted, as if his eyes were tapping an invisible calculator— "currently two thousand seven hundred and thirty-five pieces in the gallery."

"Wow." He was no maths expert, but that was a lot of money.

"And, about the tracks, they are for moving the paintings around, with an electric system. From high to low, vice versa, side to side. Sometimes I have to move the higher ones to ground level if I want to use them."

"But use them how? They're already painted?"

Dante stopped strolling. Stroking his beard, he said, "Choose a painting."

"What for?"

"Not telling. Now, please choose a painting. It is a simple request, no?"

"Any one I like?"

He nodded. "Sure, choose one that strikes you"—he placed a soft poke in the middle of Jack's chest— "right here."

"Erm, but they're all amazing?"

Slow tutting through smiling lips, he said, "Paintings speak to people in unique ways. Walk a little, look. One will speak to you, I promise."

Jack soon discovered that was true. "Dante, I've found one."

Hanging at ground level, it was one of the larger paintings. A landscape that riveted with the richness of its content. Forests, valleys and sea neighboured in exquisite balance below peaks of jagged mountains marbled in black and white; their tops reaching high into cloud-swathed sky.

But that wasn't what had spoken to Jack. The centrepiece had. It was a giant monster depicted in its stride, prowling on lush green grass. The fierceness of feather, beak, mane and talon were combined in terrifying majesty. And he couldn't walk past it.

"It's the same one from the sculpture, right? Over the palace entrance?"

Dante walked beside Jack with hands clasped behind him. His smile looked broader than his shoulders. "Wonderful, Jack. This is one of my favourites. No surprise that it spoke to you. And yes, it is indeed. You have a keen eye. I sculpted that the same as I painted this, but"—he shrugged— "my chisel is nothing like my paintbrush."

"What is it? It's so huge."

"It is a creature that *some* would say is mythological. Only alive in ancient stories from Egypt, Persia, Greece and so forth. I disagree."

"But it's a bird mixed with a cat?"

"Yes, a giant eagle and giant lion combined. A noble being of awesome strength and intelligence."

"So then, it can't be real."

Dante walked close to the canvas. Inches from its surface, inspecting. "Looks real to me. I bet you fifty pence its real."

"Deal." Jack didn't have fifty pence, but he also knew creatures like that didn't exist.

"Ok then, come and look closer," he said with a beckoning index finger.

He stood next to Dante, looking. "It's just paint. It's not real."

"You need to look *much* closer," said Dante. With that, he placed a hand on Jack's shoulder and pushed him right through the painting.

The canvas remained intact.

CHAPTER 11

Canvas pressed against Jack's face like cling film, and then burst in a puff of glittering golden sparks, sending him plunging through dazzling light. There was no pain, nothing bad, just bewilderment.

The brilliance surged and faded in a flash. He stumbled onto a soft surface. It was lush green grass. Same as in the painting.

Looking at the mountains, he recognized them from the painting too. He reached out to touch—to feel the texture of paint under his fingertips—but merely lurched forward. There was no canvas. He swiped twice at the air and struck nothing. What was going on? Jack bent and grasped two handfuls of grass. Ticklish, the soft blades bunched against his palms; their roots holding firm under the ground. It couldn't be real, could it?

Jack turned to where he'd come from and saw a glowing light suspended in the air, like the puckered head of a pomegranate. Gold and silver rays were fizzing from its tiny eye.

Then he heard a sound cannoning across the sky. A screech. Like a dozen flock of eagles calling out as one.

A plane with feathers was flying towards him from afar. The giant wings gliding steadily, they dipped and rose in slow, mighty motions. And there was nowhere to hide!

Dante's wild grey hair appeared through the beaming hole, then his body. He stepped on the grass, stretching in a backwards rowing stance. Filling his lungs, the bearded cheeks swelled in happy bunches.

"Dante, the monster's coming! We have to run!"

He strolled to beside Jack, crouching and putting a reassuring arm round his shoulder. Smiling as the creature approached ever closer. "Calm yourself, dear boy. It's not a monster. And"—he rubbed Jack's hair— "you owe me fifty pence, apprentice."

When it landed, both the ground and Jack quaked. Trying to hide behind his mentor, he said, "It'll eat us. We have to run."

"Another fifty pence says you're wrong again," said Dante; his eyes relaxed, glinting with casual confidence.

Sunflower yellow, its beak was hooked and huge, it reminded Jack of the bucket part of an industrial digger: designed to tear and devour. Its head was an eagle, but with a neck covered in dense lion's mane, the colours a sand and charcoal blend.

It came closer. Its fur-covered body was a bus with muscles. Jack could feel the ground vibrate with each step it took. The grass was flattening in broad patches under its two front talons. Divided into three, each one ended in black hooks the size of swords. Its two brown wings raised then arched backwards like yacht sails. Every feather was long as a cricket bat. A leathery tail trailed far behind, the twined sinews resembling a powerful whip.

Dante was alight with smiles. Standing, he opened his arms wide. "Old friend. Come here."

The creature brushed its enormous beak against Dante's body in soft nudges. The sound it made was a mix of purr and warble. Neither a cat nor a bird. Then it let out a squawk that made Jack jump back in fright.

Dante was stroking its mane, petting its beak. "It's ok, he's just a little grumpy, because I haven't come to see him in a while." He spoke to the massive beast like he was consoling a Chihuahua. "I'm sorry, grumpy guts, I'll try to come more often."

Semi-confident he wasn't on the menu; Jack's curiosity was now taking charge. "What is he?"

"Samonoska."

"What's a Samonoska?"

Still stroking its mane, he turned and laughed. "No, his name is Samonoska."

The creature squawked, but it was far milder than before. His blue eyes—like football-sized sapphires—had now focused on Jack. They seemed curious. Dante stretched his arm towards Jack. "Samonoska, this is Jack, my apprentice."

Samonoska cooed and hummed. It sounded like a hundred pigeons trapped inside a faulty vacuum cleaner. Dante let out a laugh while speaking to the giant eagle-lion mix. "I know, right? Finally."

He stepped back, doing a fancy bow with bended knee and outstretched leg. Pointing with both palms upwards towards his gigantic friend, he said, "Jack, let me introduce the mighty Samonoska"—he paused, raising his voice to announcement— "the King of all the Griffins."

* * *

"This is impossible!" The wind washing across them was like a Scottish summer breeze; cool, refreshing but not oppressive. What confounded Jack was that it was blowing inside a painting. And he was standing next to a giant griffin. Inside a painting.

"Says who, you?" Dante was leaning with his upper body nestled into Samonoska's mane.

"Well, yes."

"I say possible. Samonoska?" The beak opened a fraction, releasing a cluck and clack. "He agrees with me. So—"

"But how can it be?" Jack was having a real problem accepting his current reality.

"Why shouldn't it be?" Dante was patting the griffin's beak. Was its dagger-like tip bobbing in agreement?

"It's impossible! How is this possible?" Jack was insistent, the sole voice of reason trying to make sense of a startling situation. And yet the ground was firm and wind fresh.

"In time, apprentice. Now is not for how or why. Now is time for"—he stood back and pointed to the griffin's wings— "fly, fly fly."

"What?"

"He likes you, wants to take you on a tour of his world."

Jack had flown in planes twice and enjoyed it, but he wasn't keen on riding a flying lion. "You can't be serious?"

"Why not? I will be with you all the way. I've flown on him lots of times myself. There's nothing to worry about. Samonoska, if you please?"

The griffin lay its upper body flat. His tree trunk leg stretched like a ladder of fur, leading to his massive back. Dante made an ushering gesture.

"I don't think I can. I'm afraid. What if I fall off?"

Nodding, Dante's eyes searched upwards before they met with Jack's again. "Your fears are understandable, and I would never force you. But I'll make you a deal. You open to listening?"

"Well, ok."

"So, here is the deal: You fly with me on Samonoska—and by the way he would never let you fall off, nor would I—and at the end, when he brings us back here, if you are not crackling with excitement, ecstatic and begging to fly off again on his back, then"—he flicked his eyebrows alongside a sly grin— "I will give you every painting in the Gallery of Galleries."

"What? But they must be worth—"

"You would be the richest boy in the world. Easily."

"Are you being serious? You'd really give them all to me?"

"Yes. And I always keep my word. Do we have a deal?"

"But what if I pretended I didn't like it, just so I could be super rich?"

Jutting his bottom lip, he bobbed his head side to side. "Hmm. Possible. Would you do that?"

"Of course not."

He leaned close to Jack and pinched his cheek. "That was my conclusion too. Jack, I know the glint of greed in eyes when I see it. And do you know what I see in yours?" His breath smelled like sweet tobacco masked by spearmint.

"What?"

"Courage."

"Courage? I can't even sleep in the dark."

Gesturing, his puffy hair pointed to the griffin waiting for take-off. "Then fly with us and prove me wrong. Or right. The deal stands either way."

Jack clambered over the thigh and onto the back of Samonoska. The wide plateau was chiselled in bulky chunks poking from under smooth lion fur. Bumps of muscle gave little way under Jack's trainers. "Where do I sit?"

Dante pointed to the mane. "In first class. I'll sit in business, behind you."

Nervous, Jack sat with his legs dangling either side of Samonoska's colossal neck. Surprisingly silky, the mane smelled like leather and wood sprinkled in salt. The rich hair flowed over Jack's lower body like a luxury fur blanket. Samonoska's muscles contracted around Jack's legs, holding them in firm but gentle grasp, like a seatbelt. "Wow, this is like a real aeroplane."

"He wants to make sure you're happy. After so many years, he was convinced I'd never find an apprentice. He likes you a lot," Dante said as he sat behind Jack, arms sliding over and grasping two bunches of locks like they were reins on a horse.

"You won't hurt him? Grabbing his hair like that?"

"Hurt him? If I used a grenade launcher, I could perhaps bruise him. Now, are you ready?"

"As much as I'll ever be. Can you please tell him to be careful?"

Dante's thick beardy curls brushed against Jack's slender shoulder. "He already knows."

Samonoska rose. The meadow below grew smaller with every massive flap. The breeze was brisker against Jack's cheeks, and both he and Dante had to raise their voices to hear each other over the soft whistles of wind. But it was still pleasant. No shivers or shouting. He'd worried about falling off, but the tender clamp of muscle around his legs made him feel he was strapped into a pilot's seat. Every time his hands—tiny in comparison to the titan underneath him—stroked the mane, a contented hum vibrated through the griffin, sending tingles up Jack's body.

"So, are you terrified?" asked Dante with sheep curls and beard swaying in the gentle gusts Samonoska was navigating.

"I thought I would be. But I'm not? I feel like he knows how I feel. Like he even knows what I'm thinking?"

"In a way, yes. Griffins are highly intelligent

and intuitive, more than most people. And since he is the greatest of the griffins..."

"And you created him? Really?"

Eyes searching above for an answer, Dante sucked air through his teeth. "In so far as his physical appearance, yes. But"—he patted the sinewy surface they sat on— "he makes himself unique, through his personality and behaviour. I can wish things to be a particular way in the works I do, but a painting has a life of its own. Control is never complete. It's complicated, Jack. Over time, you'll have a clearer understanding. For now, enjoy the ride."

Squawking in agreement, Samonoska glided and flapped, carrying them across the sky with his mighty wings. Jack guzzled the view as verdant valleys, winding rivers and shimmering lakes all passed underneath. The world's geography was abundant and glorious.

Dipping, Samonoska swooped low, grazing tall treetops with his talons and paws. Then, banking like a feathery jumbo jet, he rose again, heading towards the sea.

Gliding mere feet above its shifting surface, his wings slapped the waves several times, drenching Jack and Dante in fountains of foam. Hair and clothes soaked, Jack wiped salty water from his face, gasping in surprise, laughing. He looked back to see Dante's beard dripping and mouth smiling. "He's showing off for you. Don't worry, we'll be dry soon enough."

They flew countless miles, circling slopes of mountains and swooping through canyons.

"What if we get lost? What if we can't find that thing we came out of? The thing with the bright lights?"

"The portal? A painter can never forget where a portal is. Relax."

"Are you sure? We've flown so far."

"Can you forget where your backside is?"

"What?"

"Your backside. Will it go walking off by itself? Will you misplace it?"

"Of course not!"

"And so it is with a painter and his portal. Besides"—he rubbed the muscley velvet they rode on— "you are with the king. Fear not."

Samonoska flew fast and time did the same. Blue gave way to black, and moon replaced sun. The stars sparkled.

"Look at the stars!" As soon as Jack spoke the griffin soared. Wings flapping in rapid flutters, they rocketed upwards. "Whoa, what's he doing?"

"Taking us closer to the stars, of course."

And that he did. The world looked more like a map when Samonoska stopped. Treading the air at first, he glided in slow circles. Jack marvelled at the sky as it glittered like black satin scattered with diamonds. "Amazing. I've never seen stars like these before."

Dante patted his shoulder. "Thanks, all my

own work."

"I'm sure I'll wake up any second."

"Don't wake up before the next part."

"What's the next part?"

"There is a universal law, Jack. The same inside or outside of paintings. Do you know what that is?"

Samonoska made humming, warbling noises. The furry muscles around Jack's legs tightened. It wasn't painful, but the grip was noticeably firmer. Dante's hands grasped the locks of mane, winding them over his knuckles and leaning forward, enclosing his arms round Jack.

"Erm, no?"

"Gravity."

The griffin's head tilted forward, and they barrelled towards the ground. Wind whooshed, mane billowed, and feathers fluttered as Jack's drawn-out shout started in fear but ended in elation. And then, with paw thuds and wing flaps, they landed safely on the ground. Back at the patch of grass where the journey had started. The fizzling gold and silver rays hanging in the air were no less bright, despite day having turned to night.

"Let's go again! Can we?" Having disembarked, Jack was beaming, running his palms up and down Samonoska's beak. It was smooth as porcelain and solid as lead. "Just one more quick ride?"

Dante's smile was kind, but his eyes looked

tired. "He will be here for next time. Say goodbye for now, Jack."

"Bye, Samonoska. Was so nice to meet you. Hope to see you soon."

A purring warble and soft squawk confirmed the same sentiment.

They walked into the dazzling rays, through the canvas and once again stood in the Gallery of Galleries. As they strolled past the other paintings to go back above ground, Dante put his arm over Jack's shoulder and said, "Just think, these would all have been yours…"

CHAPTER 12

"So, you still think you might be dreaming?" Dante was slicing and gobbling, mumbling through pieces of fried egg and sausage as his knife and fork poked and scraped the plate. Jack's mum would have been seething, had she seen it. She'd always scolded him for talking with his mouth full and making too much noise during meals.

Jack—cheeks bursting with chocolate breakfast cereal—shook his head. The mix of creamy milk and crunchy cocoa was satisfying. The lack of logical answers to all the questions in his head less so.

It was the morning after his first venture inside a painting. He was desperate to go back and see Samonoska—and then try exploring other paintings—but still troubled at the impossibility of it all. He swallowed the sugary mix and said, "Not dreaming, but..." Jack didn't want to offend his new mentor, although he got the feeling that would be hard to do.

"But?" Dante asked before taking a long slurp from his gleaming white teacup. It sounded like someone using a straw to drain the final froth from the bottom of their milkshake. His mum really wouldn't have enjoyed meals at Dante's palace. Jack giggled at the awful table manners.

"Well, it's just...crazy, isn't it?"

Dante dabbed his mouth with a napkin. Full fried breakfast had been reduced to yolk spots and crumbs of crisped bacon rind. "Crazy. Mhm. Ok. I'll let you finish your choco pops, then we can sit on the terrace and talk about it. Take your time."

The terrace looked onto remarkable gardens. Enormous green lawns were lined and separated in thick rose bushes; the petals of their pink and red badges quivering from the wind's tender kiss. Red-swathed maple branches high above formed a rustling canopy through which shards of sunlight swayed thin to thick, streaking across the ground in golden hues. Birds warbled a contented concert from the trees' eaves. It all combined into a manicured masterpiece of nature.

Jack sat in a bucket armchair with a puffy leather seat and woven frame. It was the type used for outdoor furniture and much comfier than the cheap wooden deckchairs in his garden back home. Dante, whose collarless linen shirt and trousers had not one speck of paint on them, moved his chair further away from Jack. He took an ashtray from the breakfast room and rested it on his lap. Slipping a slim silver case from his pocket, he opened it with a click and slid out a small cigar.

"I need to be more mindful of passive smoking, now you're here. There's no reason for both of us to engage in this stupid habit," he said before turning the cigar end to red ember with spark, flame and puff.

Jack had brought a glass of orange juice from the buffet. He sipped as Dante smoked. The liquid was both sweet and tart, coating his tongue in zesty fibres of orange segment. It was even nicer than cola.

"Then, why do it if it's stupid?"

Dante exhaled thick smoke, which lingered a second before billowing into the breeze. Jack caught hints of its sweet, peppery scent. It was kind of nice, he supposed.

With the cigar between his fingers, he pointed it at Jack, eyebrows raised, like a clever point had been made. "That, my dear apprentice, is the question of the ages. If something is stupid, why do we do it? After all, one might say, intentionally having stupid habits—when of course science and society have long shown them harmful—is crazy, yes?"

"Yes, seems so."

"Seems so, indeed. Let us take just three common examples: alcohol, tobacco and gambling. These things are destructive. They can harm not only us, but the people around us. They can destroy our lives. Even kill us. Yes?"

"Well, I know I'm not allowed to do any of those things because I'm too young, so they must be at least a little dangerous."

"A lot dangerous, believe me. And yet"—he puffed, the smoke snaking round his face then wisping away— "in Scotland you can use tobacco and alcohol if you are over 18 and have the money. The same goes for casinos. You can throw away health and wealth and nobody thinks anything of it. That's crazy, isn't it? But people accept it as normal."

Jack saw where Dante's logic was leading, but felt it flawed. "Yes, it's crazy, but not same as walking into a painting and doing stuff inside there. Throwing your money away is just stupid. It's not magic like you do."

His smile was broad amongst curls of bushy beard. "Magic like *we* do. But it's not really magic, in any case. We're painters, not magicians. What we do is no more unusual than sitting here right now."

"No way, sorry, that's not true, Dante."

"Is that so? Let me ask you"—Dante rested his cigar in the crystal ashtray and sprang to his feet— "where are we right now?"

"The terrace?"

"Yes"—he nodded, stretching the word, as if Jack's answer was both right and wrong— "but where is the terrace?"

"In the palace?"

His hands moved in circles, as if he were coaxing a specific answer out of Jack. "Yes, but where is the palace? And the answer isn't Scotland, or the United Kingdom."

"But we are—Oh, I see. Earth. We're on Earth."

Dante chuckled. "Right, and so?" He shrugged, palms open and spread wide.

"So what?" Jack returned the shrug.

"So that's a fact, right?"

"Of course."

Dante was stroking his beard again, looking sly, but not in a nasty way. "Anything crazy about that?"

"No, why would there be?"

He paced the terrace in slow strides, back and forth. "Of course, of course. Nothing crazy about where we are now. Oh no, not at all."

Jack looked at supple tree branches swaying in the wind and then across at the meticulously kept gardens. It was so calm and beautiful. Nothing crazy.

Dante walked closer, his hands tracing a circle in the air, coming to rest as if holding an invisible ball.

"We are standing on a giant sphere made of rock"—he stamped a sandaled foot on the terrace's stone slabs— "which floats, with nobody holding it up"—he withdrew his palms from under the imaginary globe— "and which spins"—he twirled his index finger— "with nobody spinning it. And, by the way, it is spinning right now at one thousand miles per hour as we sit here. Can you feel it?"

"One thousand? Really?" Nobody had told him that before. That *was* crazy.

"Yes, really. And this floating, spinning giant sphere is in an expanse of darkness so vast that it stretches on for"—he flailed both arms to the sky— "infinity. Or"—he shrugged— "perhaps not infinity. Nobody knows. And do you know why nobody knows?"

"No?" He didn't know, but he knew Dante knew.

"Because it stretches so far, for so many trillions and trillions of miles in every direction, nobody could possibly ever know."

"Wow, trillions? That's unreal." Billions were big enough.

"Yes, unreal. Excellent word choice, Jack. The void surrounding us stretches so far, our minds cannot even fathom it. And yet"—his voice grew soft, and he made invisible brush strokes in the air like it was a canvas— "I create paintings, that I happen to walk inside and enjoy—just as we are doing now on this floating, spinning rock you casually call Earth—and you say it's...crazy?"

The last word left Dante's lips in a delicate whisper.

Jack found himself re-examining the definition of crazy.

CHAPTER 13

Paint carpeted the floorboards. Decades—Jack guessed—of unintended spills and splashes caused by his new teacher's flamboyance. Chaos in colour marbled underneath Jack's trainers as he took in the latest palace location.

Breathing deeply, he noticed there was no cigar smell in the air, only hints of paint fume. No ashtrays either. The only room so far not to have them, except his bedroom.

They were in the studio, where Jack was unleashing a tempest of questions. And it seemed to delight Dante. In fact, every excited inquiry appeared to lift his mentor's level of elation further.

Except he hadn't answered. Instead, he was looking out of the enormous bay windows, smiling and nodding with his black sandals planted in elongated tiles of light. Sunshine was making full use of its licence to roam around the room.

The place looked tiny compared to the Gallery of Galleries, but its ceiling was still higher than most houses. The window side—the one Dante now admired the view from—was a giant semi-circle of steel and glass, looking onto lavish gardens. Jack wasn't focused on flowers and trees now though. He wanted answers.

"Dante, are you listening?"

He turned to Jack; his beard bathed in rays. "Of course, my dear boy. Sorry, so many questions. Questions from an enthusiastic apprentice. They are invigorating, like symphonies. But yes, we must begin untangling the riddles that—understandably—agitate you. Now, where shall we start?"

"Well, did you know I had a…gift when you looked at the drawing my dad sent you?"

He leaned into a light perch on the windowsill and shook his head. "Not exactly. There was something that appealed to me about your work. It didn't scream at me like your bananas, but I saw potential. Potential should be given proper investigation. However—"

"And the other candidates? Did they all send you paintings? And did you see something in them?"

"They all sent me paintings, but to be quite honest, I saw the same from their first entries as I did from their efforts in the amphitheatre:

extreme artistic talent and nothing more. They were brilliant—perhaps one or two of them might even be termed geniuses—but at no time did I see anything that hammered my eyeballs and set my brain ablaze."

"Then why invite them all the way up here if you knew they didn't have what you were looking for?"

"As I was trying to say a moment ago, for almost four decades I haven't been entirely sure *what* I was looking for. I know what my own work is, but I've never been sure what the gift might look like reflected in the paintings of others. After all, I've never seen anything else. All I knew was, I would recognize it when I saw it. So yes, as with all the other candidates before them, I—despite being less than optimistic—offered substantial money to inspect their efforts while the paint was being brushed fresh in front of me. I didn't know if that would make a difference or not? When you search for something so unique, so precious, you leave nothing to chance. Jack"— he gave Jack's arm a soft squeeze and rub— "I have spent my whole life searching for another like myself. And after so much time in that type of situation, one becomes increasingly desperate. Do you understand?"

"I think so. You were losing hope?"

"Exactly. I'm not getting any younger. I didn't want my knowledge to die with me. But"— his cheeks bunched as he brushed a tobacco-tinged palm over Jack's cheek— "my determination paid off, eh?"

"I suppose so. But am I really...like you? I don't think I could do something that amazing. Making living creatures? And mountains and stars and—"

"You didn't think you could fly across the sky on the back of a giant griffin, but you did, didn't you?"

"Yes, true." That was no small feat, for sure. "But that's being brave, not magical."

"Sometimes bravery is more difficult to summon than magic. Trust me on that. Now"— he nodded towards a blank canvas resting on sturdy easels in the studio's centre— "perhaps the best way to dispel doubts is to dive straight in?"

"Painting? Already?" Jack had thought it would be weeks or even months before he'd be allowed to do his own proper one. Now he knew what painting truly meant; the thought frightened him.

Dante patted the air with palms, as if pushing down an excited springer spaniel. "Calm down, dear apprentice. Relax. I'm talking about something simple."

"How simple? What should I paint?"

He stroked his beard. The sunlight was surging against his linen-clad shoulders. "As simple as you like. And you tell me. It's your painting."

Jack focused on what might be simple and

—hopefully—harmless. "A snowman?" He'd only played in snow once. They didn't get it much in London. He had happy memories of calm, fluttering fluff though.

Nodding slowly with eyes breaking into smile, Dante said, "Yes, yes. I like it. But may I suggest a slight change?"

"What's that?"

"Snow."

"Snow?"

"Yes, snow. Without the man. You can paint the snow, which will be extremely simple, then enter the painting and literally build the snowman from your own work. What do you think?"

Making a snowman sounded fun, especially in the middle of summer. "Ok, sure. Will you help me?"

"Build the snowman? Of course." His face was a mask of mischief.

"Well, yes that too, but I meant paint. I don't know what to do."

Walking towards the corner, Dante pulled a trolley laden with paints and brushes beside the canvas. The wheels squeaked as they rolled across myriad miniscule bumps. "I really must get this floor re-done. It's getting ridiculous. Yes"—he turned to Jack and stood with hands on hips— "I will guide you. But, before you start, I must ask: How do you feel?"

"I feel fine."

"So, you're happy? Anything troubling

you?"

"I'm happy. I'm a little nervous about painting, but I'll be ok if you're here."

He flicked his hand backwards like swatting away a fly. "A little nervous is ok. I will be here to help, so don't worry. But, just to be clear, there's nothing churning deep in your stomach? Like sadness? Anger? Nothing bad at all?"

Dante was peering like a doctor performing diagnosis.

"No, I feel good." Jack sensed the questioning was about more than his settling in at the palace. "Would feeling bad make painting a problem?"

Dante lifted one of the largest brushes from the trolley and flipped through its beige bristles with his fingertip. Then he held it out to Jack, who took it by its tapered handle. The wood was peanut colour, with a gleaming strip of metal connecting it to the brush part. The whole thing was surprisingly spotless, considering the state of the floor.

"First, tell me, what is that?" Dante asked.

Cradling the brush across two palms, Jack replied, "A brush for broad strokes? It looks like the thick bristles can carry a lot of paint, but I doubt it's useful for doing fine detail."

The way Dante nodded— conceding the facts but without satisfaction —told Jack a deeper answer was needed. "You learn fast, but there is something more to it."

"Erm, it's like a magic wand?"

Lips pursed and cheeks bulging, he let loose a sputtering wheeze. "Magic wand? Who do you think you are? You're not a wizard, Jack." The tone was gentle, his teasing without nastiness.

Jack giggled, holding the brush up and pointing at Dante, saying, "Abracadabra."

He pretended to shield, shouting in fake alarm, "Careful, you'll turn me into a chicken or a goblin."

After a good few minutes of joint laughter, his smile eased into seriousness. "It is a powerful instrument when in your hands. It not only creates life through paint but is a conductor." He picked up another brush, one much smaller, and grazed the canvas with its tip.

"A conductor? Like with electrical stuff?"

"Excellent, Jack. Think of the paintbrush like that type of conductor, and your thoughts and emotions the electricity. When you paint"— he ran his fingertip from shoulder to brush — "the feelings and thoughts in your body are transmitted along the brush and"—he tapped on the canvas— "end up in the painting. As you paint the physical pictures, that which can be seen, you send your wishes for what cannot be seen. For example, you might paint a garden full of beautiful flowers, and wish for them to smell particularly delightful. Or if you are allergic, you might wish for the flowers not to have pollen. Or you might wish for whoever tends the flowers to be friendly, or to be a fantastic storyteller. In any case, just as in the real world, positive energy and thoughts encourage good things, while negativity spreads and damages like a poison, causing problems."

"What kind of problems?"

He slid up his linen sleeve and nodded at the scars, wrapped like crimson ribbons round his caramel skin. "Big ones."

CHAPTER 14

"So, my dear apprentice it seems we have our first disagreement early on, eh?" he spoke like he was poking with a sharpened pencil.

Surrounded by an endless expanse of ankle-deep snow, they stood on a patch criss-crossed with crisply compressed shoe prints.

"I know it's rude, but I really do feel I'm right in this case," said Jack with arms folded in defiance.

Dante stroked his beard with cotton-coated fingers and breathed in frosty billows. "Is that so?"

Jack had painted with ease—and to enthusiastic praise—with Dante telling him to wish in his heart what the characteristics of the snow would be. As his brushstrokes coated the canvas in white, Jack had imagined thick stuff, soft as feathers. Safe and fluffy, not icy.

Once the painting was complete, they'd changed into ski jackets and other warm clothing before entering their winter expedition. Using a small set of steps, they'd been met by soft crunches underfoot, and refreshing chill in the air. It had been simple. Like walking into a back garden through brief brightness and golden fizzle. Not scary at all.

But the smiles had disappeared. Scowl now faced off against frown as opinions collided, neither one of them wanting to concede. It was an unexpected stand-off between genius and novice.

They were arguing over who had made the best snowman.

Jack was trying not to chuckle at Dante's bad acting. "Mine is better. The two big snowballs are perfectly round. Yours are...like sausage rolls?" said Jack, enjoying the freedom of cheekiness to an adult.

Palms out in appeal, Dante pointed to his snowman. "Sausage roll? You must be—ok, maybe a little like sausage roll—but, my dear boy, the devil is in the details, no? Look at the nose, it's much nicer than your man's. And the buttons on his—"

"Only because you took the nicer carrot, and the bigger pieces of coal. That was easy. Mine would be like that if I'd been quicker to pick them up." He liked being able to talk back without fear.

Dante nodded, shrugging. "Fine, since you

painted all this wonderful snow for us to compete with, I'll give you the victory, but"—he pointed an index upwards— "I demand a rematch at some point in the future. Deal?"

"Sure, deal."

"And we had a different agreement too, yes?"

"Yea, we sure did."

"If you made the better snowman, I said I would tell you the full story about my experience"—he paused, eyelids narrowing— "with wolves."

"Yep, yes please." Jack was a fan of stories, and this was one was going to be great.

"Very well. After lunch. Now"—he clapped his palms together with a cottony thump—let's go eat."

❋ ❋ ❋

"This is a cautionary tale. Do you know what that means?" asked Dante as he leaned into the marble bench, stretching legs and crossing sandals. Streams of smoke flowed from his nostrils as he patted his stomach and sighed. Sweet spicy tobacco lingered in the leafy garden alcove where they sat.

Jack was perched on the chunky ledge of a fountain in the alcove's circular centre, its watery tinkles streaming from a stone lady holding a jug that never emptied. Wet flecks dotted his t-shirt as he drew his hand back and forth through the pool. He liked the water's cool resistance against his palm.

Full of fish and chips—the best ones he'd had in his life—he'd been waiting with contented belly as Dante puffed his cigar, gazing at the hazy blue above. Occasional tweets drifted from the trees. That and the water's patter had been the only breaks in a comfortable silence.

But now Dante was ready to begin his story. Taking his hand from the fountain's basin and wiping both sides on denim, Jack shuffled on the ledge. This was going to be awesome. "Is it a kind of warning?"

"Yes, a warning. Good, Jack. And why do you think old guys like me are always giving tales of warning to young guys like you?"

He rubbed his trainer treads across the cobbles, pausing, wanting to give the best answer. "Hmm, so we don't get in trouble?"

"Yes, correct, but why not just tell you directly to stay out of trouble?"

"I'm not sure? Because old guys like to tell stories?"

Dante laughed, easing his torso into a more upright position, but with legs still outstretched.

"I think that's part of it. But, let me ask you"—he took another puff— "if a snake—let's say a deadly cobra—slithers into this area right now, is that trouble?"

"Oh yes, definitely. Cobras are dangerous. I wouldn't want to meet one."

"You certainly wouldn't. Now, if a man walks in here, smiling, polite, and kindly offers you, say, I don't know—what's your favourite ice cream?"

"Mint choc chip, and you?"

"Pistacchio, I'm a traditional old Italian. Anyway, not important. So, this polite, smiling man offers you mint choc chip, free of charge. Is that trouble?"

"No? He's just being nice, right?"

Dante puffed, speaking through wisps of smoke. "Maybe. Maybe it's a simple act of kindness. But maybe"—he tapped his cigar ash onto the cobbles— "he is a snake that smiles. Far more dangerous than the one that slithers. The cobra attacks on instinct; we know what it is, and we can flee. But the smiling snake masks his venom in good manners. He chooses his time to strike. We might not know that until it's too late. How can you tell the difference if you don't have experience with this type of unseen trouble?"

"By learning from people who do have experience," replied Jack.

Dante nodded, his bearded cheeks bunching. "Good, good. And one of the best ways for anybody to increase wisdom is—at least in my opinion—by listening to stories. So, with that in mind, let me tell you of my experience with wolves." He stared towards the hedging but neither at it nor through it. Letting out a slow exhale through circled lips, he said, "How the time flies. It really does seem like yesterday. The day I discovered—almost to my demise—that using my gift was not without its risks. I was a boy. Older than you, but still a boy. I think eighteen, no, nineteen, and I had been trying hard to impress a young lady—"

Jack giggled. "What was her name?"

"Violetta," said Dante with his delicate Italian accent dancing out the syllables.

"Wow, that's a nice name. Was she pretty?"

He bunched fingertips at his lips and flared them into the air with a kiss. "Bellissima! An angel like no other. And her looks were unusual for an Italian girl: red hair, eyes like emeralds, skin pale as milk. If I close my eyes"—he did exactly that, breathing deeply— "I can still see the tiny freckles across the bridge of her nose. Anyway"—he opened his eyes and took another puff— "suffice to say she caught the eyes of other suitors, so—"

"What's a suitor?"

"It's someone who likes another person—in a romantic way—and begins making efforts to capture that person's heart. Usually with marriage in mind."

"So, you were also her suitor?"

"Yes, I was but"—he shrugged, lips pursed and palms outwards— "I failed in my attempts."

"Why?"

"Girls like that have lots of suitors, lots of options. They're usually spoiled for choice, in fact. And I was not what she wanted."

"Why not?" Jack couldn't imagine Dante as a young man, but he must have always been clever and funny.

"After many months of my pursuing her, she told me plainly—not rudely but plainly—that I was not suitable. She wanted an alpha male and told me so. Sadly, I have never been that type of man."

"Wha—"

"Alpha is a dominant male. In Italy at that time, it meant a macho man, a tough guy with muscles. One who could use his aggression and fists, to dominate other men. But I was a painter, not a fighter. I had wild hair and wild ideas, but not a wild streak in that way. And so, she chose another man. Not the right man for her—at least in my opinion—but that was her choice."

Water babbled and birds warbled as the story continued with Dante's voice softer, more distant.

"I gave up chasing her and retreated to my studio. And, in my sadness, I painted; the largest and most challenging work I had tried up to that point. I decided I would escape into a place where

I could prove my masculinity, even if she would never see it. I would prove it to myself."

"What did you paint?"

"Mountains, meadows, forests, a shining sea, and a fearsome creature which I could ride across the heavens, declaring dominance over the world I had made."

"No! Samonoska?"

Dante nodded. "The one and only."

"Really? Then where did the wolves come from? I didn't see any wolves in there, thank God." Jack couldn't believe he'd walked on the same grass where the story—a true and scary story—had happened.

"Nor would you. Now"—he sucked on the cigar, held it and breathed out slow, smoky billows— "while painting the King of the Griffins, I felt wondrous joy. His majesty and strength were inspiring, uplifting. My happiness thrived, tickled, sending tingles along all my fingers and toes. So that was great. No issues there. But, at other times, while brushing blades of grass to form the meadows, or smudging waves of that shimmering sea, I would recall Violetta's words, dismissing me, shattering my hopes of capturing her heart. Self-doubt would grasp, then release, only to repeat. I felt annoyance at myself that I wasn't a man of dominant nature in the real world, an alpha. That was what the beauties seemed to crave."

"But you were creating a whole new world.

A real world! That's miles better than having big muscles or being able to bully other men around, just to impress a pretty girl."

"Logic screams that to be the case." The cigar had burned down to his fingernails. He laid it in the groove between two cobbles, then slid another one from his silver case and lit it, puffing away. "But the mind of a young man is not always logical, especially when beautiful girls are involved."

"I don't really see the fuss about girls. I hope I won't act silly over them when I grow up."

"Ha! We shall see soon enough, I think. Now, the wolves—"

"Yes, the wolves," said Jack, shifting forward on the stone ledge. This was the good bit.

"I entered through that same portal you did. The grass was just as green as when you stood on it, the mountains no less awesome. I breathed the air; it was fresh, clean. But Samonoska, as you know yourself, likes to stretch his wings. He was nowhere to be seen. So, I decided to walk through the meadows, enjoying the chatter of birds and flutter of butterflies, calling out the name I had given him. Breeze kissed my forehead, sun warmed my back, and alpine grandeur caressed my eyes. It was wonderful"—he bolted upright with sandals planted on the ground, his tone sharpening— "until it wasn't."

"The attack?"

"Yes. At first, I heard howling from afar. The

eery pitches of a ravenous pack. I was shocked. I had neither painted wolves nor wished for them in that world as my brushes stroked the canvas. They—of course—hadn't been visible on the finished painting and I had stepped through in ignorance of the danger."

"But how could they be there if you didn't paint them and didn't wish them into your work?"

"The turmoil of my emotions had created them. Unseen trouble had transmitted along the brush and into the painting. And now it was real."

"Oh my God."

"That was my thought at the time, too. So, the howling stopped, but worse was on the way. They surged from the forest, circling me in a steady advance, snarling, growling. Grey, white, black; the furs varied but the fangs did not. Their jaws were jagged cemeteries, lined in white knives glistening with saliva. And then—"

"How many were there?"

Dante blew a popped puff of breath, his eyes weaving in calculation. "Fifty? Sixty? It was hard to count, especially as they had given me a strong urge to visit the bathroom." He snorted, the bushy curls rising into a smile. "I can laugh about it now, but at the time it was not a laughing matter. Aside from the terror of death, I feared I would die a fool. I had intended to make myself feel better by being the big man of that world.

And there I was, about to become its dinner."

"Oh my God. That's so many wolves. It must have been terrible. And then?"

"And then the alpha of the pack lunged, sinking his teeth into my arm. With his neck and bite combined in such vicious sinew, I thought I would be literally torn limb from limb. I was screaming, hammering with my free fist on his nose, clawing at his eyes, but to no avail. The pain stabbed like daggers. I thought it was all over"—he slapped his palm hard on the marble, causing Jack to flinch— "until it wasn't."

"Samonoska came?"

"There was a bellowing screech; thunder raging from a terrible throat. It knocked the alpha's ears flat in shock, and he released his jaws, startled. The ground shook. And before me, an enormous beak"—he formed pincers with fingers and thumb— "plucked the wolf like a chicken feather, dragging him upwards to his doom. There was a horrible crunch—though it was music to my ears, truth be told—and the headless carcass was catapulted across the meadow, landing in a bloody pile of splintered bone and twisted limbs."

"Wow! I wish I'd been there to see him fight. That would—"

"Trust me, you don't. And the battle was far from over. The other wolves tried to rally. They were great in number and not easily scared off, not even by Samonoska. They attacked him from all sides."

"What happened?"

"It was not pretty. Perhaps I should simply say his world is free of wolves now..."

Jack let out a huff and tiny whine. "But I need to know what happened."

Leaning forward, he took a long puff and rubbed his cigar's tip on the cobbles, placing the two charred stubs side by side. "Sorry, Jack. I will not go into further gruesome details, or you may have nightmares tonight. Suffice to say, there was carnage; the rampage of a newly awoken titan, revelling in the power I had given him. I was extremely thankful he was friend and not foe."

"Me too, I don't think anybody could beat him in a fight."

"On that we agree. So, sadly, it seems the greatest enemy lies within for people with our gift. To avoid these types of calamities, you must always paint with joy, or at least the absence of any major negativity. If negative emotions bubble within you, go do something else until you feel happy enough to paint. Better that than end up in a nightmare of your own making. Now, let's go back." He stood, stretching his arms up and out.

Jack slid off the fountain's ledge and they began walking down the path towards the palace. "So, what do you do if you want to paint, but you feel sad and it won't go away?"

"Me? I shout. Scream if necessary."

"Scream?"

"Yes, to cleanse the soul. I shout, scream and curse, to purge the unwanted emotions; until my body exhausts and I feel calm. It works wonders, believe me."

"When you do that, don't the palace staff think you're...crazy?"

Dante shrugged, putting a careful arm around Jack's shoulder as they walked. "No more than usual."

CHAPTER 15

The years passed.

Lambs pranced in spring; rays, rain and rainbows bathed the summer, green grew auburn in autumn and winter flakes fluttered. Eight times over.

Jack got bigger.

On the cusp of adulthood, he was no longer a little squirt. His skinny limbs had lengthened, bolstered with lean muscle. Square jaw replaced baby cheeks and previously puny torso now twitched with athletic vigour. The pitch of his voice had sunk; gentle in tone, but with underlying firmness of masculinity. His hair and eyes were still raven and hazel, but nothing else remained of the boy.

He'd grown to a young man. And a handsome one at that.

Dante was now more blend of father and friend than mentor. His beard was no less thick, but grey had outgrown black, and the wild puffs on his head were withered, thinning to wisps hidden under a fisherman's wool cap.

Jungles, lost cities, oceans and more; together they adventured throughout the Gallery of Galleries. Dante taught and guided with purpose. Jack's painting skills flourished, verging on mastery.

Jack and Samonoska's friendship grew strong. The titan was at his most contented when soaring through the sky with the young apprentice on his back.

In all that time, not a word was heard from his biological father, Arthur.

That suited Jack.

CHAPTER 16

Silky steel melodies floated through salty breeze. Drummers beat dimples within shimmering cylinders; their feet bouncing and smiles beaming in sync with metallic chimes as the crowd sunbathed, snacked, flirted and drank. Lovely ladies in bikinis lounged, sipped and laughed. Hunks in trunks and vests chatted and strutted, flexing oiled pecs and biceps.

Sweeping, bustling, and bathed in honey hues, the pool area was spread over multiple lagoons, all lined in swaying palm trees and centred with swim up bars. Romp and splash blended with merry shouts of "cheers" and clinks of glass as straws were sucked and maraschino cherries chewed. Sunglasses glinted, speckled across waves of happy holidaymakers. Everything was bright, pastel and pretty.

Jack was revelling in the atmosphere.

The resort's beach club was next to the swimming pools. Neither empty nor teeming, it had a comfortable vibe of liveliness without being overcrowded. He and Dante were at the quieter end, lying on sun loungers across from each other. Dante sheltered under a parasol in shorts and open shirt; him bronzing his physique in swim trunks and suntan lotion. Jack had positioned his lounger so he could see the steel band and beyond, but also enjoy the beach panorama.

"Is this place nice or what?" asked Jack while sipping tangy pineapple smoothie and exchanging smiles with two tanned ladies passing by in loud orange and lime.

"Yes, indeed. It has vibrance, I like it. What a fantastic location to take a break. Thank you for this, my boy," replied Dante, slurping pina colada through a thick, striped straw.

"You're welcome, Da—Dante. But…"

"What?"

"Nah, it's nothing, really." He pressed his chic designer aviators back to the top of his nose and tried to wave his words away with a casual hand flap.

"When I hear someone say it's nothing, I know for sure it's something. Now, speak. You're still my apprentice, officially. So, tell me." His sunglasses were tortoise shell retro with mirrored pink shades. So garish. Typical Dante, but then that was one of the things Jack loved about him.

Jack sighed, sitting up and planting his feet into the soft sand. It was toast warm under his bare soles. "Fine, if you insist. It's just, I mean, look it's clear you don't give a damn what people think about you, right? And I think that's great—"

"So, what's the problem then?" Dante took out his gold cigar case—the silver one having been accidentally dropped down a chasm in ancient Peru—and slid one out. His first puff was deep, the exhale savoured.

"I just wonder why you always wear that daft fisherman's hat all the time now? It's never off your head. I get the feeling it's not a fashion statement. It's not, is it?"

"Of course not. I don't like the fact I'm damn near bald. That—"

"Then why don't you just paint yourself a thick head of hair while we're in places like this?" Jack asked, gesturing to the large satchel resting in the sand beside Dante's lounger. Sturdy leather, it was sealed by two thick straps with robust golden buckles. Inside it was a full range of brushes, paints, a palette and palette knife, for any in-painting touch ups that might be necessary or helpful on their expeditions. Dante used them with breath-taking flair and ease. Jack was catching up to him, gradually.

"Because, as you well know, paint cannot leave paintings. So, if I were to follow your advice, each time we stepped back into the Gallery of Galleries I would have to endure the humiliation of hair loss. Repeatedly. You want me to feel bad at the end of each outing?" The tone was coated in mild scold and no more. Dante rarely got more than irritated at the teenager in Jack.

"No, of course not. I'm sorry, I didn't think of it that way. I just thought it seemed silly to be so self-conscious over it. You didn't seem to care about your hair before, so—"

"I did care, I just liked it wild and free, thank you very much. And silly? It's easy for you to say, at eighteen years old. Look at you, in the prime of your life. Hmm?"—he nodded at Jack's chiselled abdominals— "You know, you'll never have muscles like Jaheem, so I suggest you stop trying to follow his gym routine."

Jack saw a wry smile nestled between grey curls and felt reassured by the teasing in Dante's voice. He was glad he hadn't upset him. Flexing his biceps, feeling swelling fibres tightening against his skin, Jack replied, "Yea well, it's what the ladies like, right?"

Dante sighed. "The ladies, the ladies. Whatever, just remember what I've told you countless times before: the—"

"The true beauty is on the inside. Yep, I know. I'll eh"—his eyes caught the smouldering gaze of a slender blonde in a pink gingham onepiece— "not forget."

Tutting, and taking a deep drink from his

creamy yellow cocktail, he said with slurp and chirp, "Good lad. Glad you always listen. Now if you don't mind, perhaps you could shut your pie hole about my headwear and let me enjoy the sea in peace."

That seemed like a reasonable request. In front of them was the glorious Caribbean. A sparkling expanse, its steady flow of waves started from afar, like aquatic pulse; their tops curling and cascading, they ended in surges of bubbling froth, landing on the smooth sand shore in gentle crashes.

After a good fifteen minutes, Dante leaned forward, peering at the marbled plateaus of freshly mashed water as they retreated, fizzing, towards the sea. "Hmm, periwinkle and aquamarine. Not bad. Although a little teal wouldn't have hurt, but not bad"—he took a short sip from his straw— "not bad at all."

"Thanks, I know you like a nice sea view, so I took extra care with it."

"Good job. You'll be a master before you know it. You want a top up?"

"Nah, I'm good thanks. Plus, you know I wished the whole resort all-inclusive when I was painting it, right? The bar's just across there. It's all free."

"This is more fun, and I'm a better mixologist than any of those bartenders." His glass empty, Dante opened both the satchel and bamboo box inside it, taking out a small brush for fine detail. Dipping it in paint, he hunched over so the flicks and swirls were hidden from others on the beach. Then he placed the tools and box back inside the satchel and re-buckled the straps.

"Ah, that's better. I like my pina coladas extra cold." The glass's straight sides were misty with thick frost and the drink was chinking with chunky ice cubes. Jack caught wafts of rum between the pineapple and coconut. He must have painted an extremely strong one.

"It's incredible how you do that. How on earth do you do it so fast? I feel like it takes me ages to paint inside these places."

"Skills are rarely perfect, but decades of practice can help you get close. One of the few benefits of old age. If it makes you feel any better, you're pace of learning is astonishing. You have grasped the concept of painting the canvas that surrounds you"—he waved his hand back and forth through the air— "far faster than myself at eighteen. Another year and you might even be as good as me. But..." Lengthening of the last word hinted at the start of a mini lecture.

"But...?" Jack's wavy raven fringe was fluttering. He welcomed the lukewarm washes of air against his forehead.

"Don't get careless, or cocky, or start showing off to people within the worlds you craft. When you paint internally, be discreet, so as not to attract attention."

"I don't show off"—he pointed with two indexes at his Spartan torso— "except for this, of course."

"No, you don't, but I still remember my time as a teenager, even though it was long ago. The need to be accepted, recognized, admired, adored, especially by the ladies that distract you so much. I see it in you, and I sometimes worry, Jack," said Dante.

"Don't worry, please. I'll do what you tell me. Even though I don't think all of it makes sense for people like us."

Dante was stirring the ice cubes with his straw. Frost on the glass was melting in patches, the sides already crying with condensation from his firm clasp. Pinching sand playfully between his hairy toes, he asked "Mhm, and who are people like us, exactly?"

"Never mind. I don't want to get into it."

"Why do I get the feeling you do want to get into it, just that you suspect I will disagree with you?"

"What's the point in talking about something we won't agree on?"

"Likelihood of disagreement doesn't mean the topic isn't worth discussing. Tell me your thoughts and tell them fully. Go on."

"Ok then, fine. Look, you know I don't like to brag—"

"Which means you are about to brag. Humble brag, I suspect. Mhm ok, go on."

Jack sputtered a chuckle and shook his head.

It was difficult trying to debate anything with Dante. "I mean, I created all of this"—he gestured around the beach with open palms— "everything in it, apart from us and our gear, of course. The hotel, all these people, the beach. I even made the Caribbean—obviously, not the real Caribbean, but still—that's not bragging, that's just a fact."

Dante nodded, taking his lips from the straw. "A fact, yes. And your point is?"

"Well, I feel like—don't get annoyed, please—being able to do these kinds of things, being the only people who can do them, as far as we know at least, that it makes us kind of"—he bobbed his head side to side— "like gods, doesn't it? I'm just being honest about it. I know this kind of discussion irritates you, but in terms of creating, we are the gods in this situation, aren't we? Why should we hide ourselves? I don't understand why we always pretend to be ordinary people in every painting we go into, except when we visit Samonoska, of course."

Placing his drink on the rattan beach table next to him, Dante slid another cigar from the gleaming case, rasped a flame and puffed until the tobacco was glowing red. Jack wished he wouldn't smoke so heavily, but he'd given up trying to persuade him away from ingrained habits. "You are right," he said after blowing out two quivering smoke rings.

"What?" asked Jack with his head jerking back. He wondered if the band's tinkling calypso rhapsodies had interfered with his hearing. "You agree with me?"

"Yes"—smoke seeped from between his grey whiskers, disappearing into the sea breeze— "we are *like* gods. But we are not gods. You—"

"What? I don't—"

"I am speaking now, young man. Be quiet and listen. You may answer when I ask you a question, ok? Stop talking."

"Fine." Jack sighed and glugged two mouthfuls of pineapple juice. He'd wished the sun a little too hot while brushing it among the blue of his canvas.

"As I was saying, you are eighteen years old. You have no health problems. You've built up your body and all the ladies smile at you. Perhaps you feel like a god now. It's understandable, but do you think those young men over there don't feel like gods too?" He pointed discreetly to a group of muscular lads standing at the nearest bar, swaggering and smiling in swim trunks and flip-flops.

"Is that a rhetorical question?"

"No. Answer me, please."

"They probably do, of course, but it's different. They're just young and healthy. They didn't make this entire world. I did." Jack spoke in strained tone, trying to push his logic into Dante's brain. He was perfectly aware of all the facts, so why didn't he agree with Jack's point of view?

"You're right. They didn't create this world and you certainly did, but"—Dante took off his sunglasses and leaned forward with voice lowering close to whisper— "they will live in it long after you and I are dead. If we will die and they will live forever, just as all these people here will live forever—assuming nobody destroys your painting—then who are the true gods in this situation? Hmm?"

He had a point. Jack hadn't carefully considered the fact his creations would all outlive him. Long outlive him. Every one of them. "I hadn't thought of it like that. But what if we stayed in here—or any of the paintings, come to think of it—forever? What if we-repainted and wished ourselves young and healthy every day, day after day?"

Dante looked downwards, stretching his spindly legs and turning them so Jack could see the network of varicose blue in his calves and ankles. "As my youth faded, I began experimenting, seeing if I could do exactly that: defy the aging process by staying in painted worlds for extended periods of time. It was futile. The aesthetic was refreshed but my inner parts were not. The most wishful of brushstrokes won't work on the human heart. It has a maximum number of beats, no matter where it is."

"We can create eternity, but we're not eternal ourselves. Doesn't seem fair."

Dante's eyes smiled. "Come here." He beckoned with wrinkly fingers. Jack leaned forward and got a firm kiss on his crown before Dante cupped his cheek, saying, "There is nothing fair in life for anyone else, so why should we be different? We are temporary visitors in the works we create, just as we are temporary on planet Earth. You and I are better than nobody. Not inside a painting nor outside. That is one of two reasons we don't glorify ourselves as painters."

"And what's the other reason?"

"Never assume people will react well to the truth."

CHAPTER 17

Dante was in the studio and a solemn mood.

"So, this was a worthy practice run. Impressive. However, your next piece should be without flaw. Do you think you're ready?"

They'd been discussing the Caribbean resort. Sea shining, hotel swanky and people pretty; its vibrance was unchanged from the previous week's visit. But now the scene was frozen on canvas, framed for eternity in gold-leaf and oak, the world within held up by heavy-duty wooden easels. Jack had titled the painting De Luca De Luxe in—slightly cheeky—recognition of his adopted father and friend, causing raised eyebrows but nothing more.

Dante coughed into his closed fist twice, pausing and massaging his chest. That damn tobacco. Jack had often considered hiding Dante's cigars, but there were too many servants who could simply bring him new boxes.

"Are you ok?" asked Jack. The grimace on Dante's face was lingering.

"Yes, yes," he said with a dismissive flick of his backhand before straightening again. "Let's focus on your upcoming work. So, are you ready?"

"I won't repeat my mistakes. I'm ready. Are you sure you're ok?"

"Yes, I'm fine. Don't fuss like an old woman. Ok then, I will have this one taken to the Gallery of Galleries and from tomorrow you will begin considering your masterpiece," said Dante as he drifted towards the window area. Onslaught from above was hammering the glass in waves of watery slaps. Dazzling streaks flashed across charcoal clouds with angry rumbles hot on their heels.

"Take a few days to mull the project over first. Then, prepare yourself with the happiest of hearts and paint with honour, wishing the finest things as your brush conducts them onto the canvas. And Jack"—he rasped hard twice, staring into the storm and speaking from the side of his mouth— "your masterpiece symbolizes the end of your apprenticeship. It is an important milestone in your life. Please choose subject matter which reflects that seriousness. I don't want to see pretty ladies in bikinis, no matter how perfectly you paint them. Is that clear?"

"Yes, understood. Although I'll be honest: I'm not sure what to choose."

"Something meaningful to you. I suggest something dear to your heart, so the emotions you have while painting will be particularly positive. You want the image on the canvas to be masterful, but likewise with the unseen aspects, within the world below its surface. They must be well wished and equally wonderful. That is a true masterpiece." He coughed yet again, rubbing his chest, thick crinkles forming round his eyes as he blew out a soft groan.

Jack was going to call the palace doctor but didn't want to make it sound like fussing. "Whatever I paint, I promise you'll be proud of me. Now, I think maybe we should get Doctor Crawford to —"

"I am already"—he rasped again, even harder this time— "proud of you. This is not about my pride. I believe in your—" He stumbled forward, trying to brace himself against the steel window frame, his chest heaving with violent wheezing.

Jack lunged, catching him as he collapsed to his knees with a sharp gasp.

* * *

Jack had never drunk alcohol before. He'd never liked the look, the smell, the way it made people behave. Didn't like anything about it.

But now he needed it.

Choosing a random decanter from the silver tray, he unplugged its square top, picked it up and poured into a glass tumbler. The crystal bottle was heavy in his grasp—heavier than it should have been—as its neck chattered against the tumbler's rim.

Ruby liquid spilling over in drips and splashes, he brought the glass to his mouth cupped in two hands. The vapours smelled like grape juice gone bad. He gagged after the first mouthful—his throat was choked by unnatural heat—but then, exhaling strongly, he ignored his discomfort and gulped the remaining alcohol. It was sweet, rich, like watered down syrup. His insides smouldered. He refilled and repeated before stumbling to a sofa with his third drink in hand. Leaning against the sofa's chunky leather arm, his nerves were slowly numbing but nowhere near pacified.

Dante was gone.

Taken from him without warning, he'd died in Jack's arms. There was no chance to say goodbye. No chance to say anything.

He was gone.

CHAPTER 18

Jack owned a palace. Jack was a billionaire. Jack was young, healthy and handsome—he was drowning in sadness.

It had been ten days since Dante passed away. He was to be cremated that afternoon. Jack was still resisting the new reality.

He and Miss Karlsson were sitting in Dante's office. The air was musty with tobacco odours. Years of nicotine and tar ingrained within the furnishings. Leaning on Dante's desk, he tried to find room for his forearms amid all the papers and stationery. He'd preserve the disorder as best he could.

Growing up, Jack had developed a crush on Dante's personal assistant. Towering, with strong limbs and striking features, she was a Nordic amazon of distinction. Her fresh floral scent and clacking heels were always a welcome presence around the palace corridors. Normally business-like, she radiated quiet sternness, even when smiling. Now though, the ice in her blue irises was melting, liquid pooling on the rims of her eyelids.

"So, to be clear, he left absolutely everything to me?" He should have been excited. He'd have swapped it all to have his friend sitting there instead.

"Yes, absolutely everything. He instructed me to have his will changed a couple of years ago. He loved you so much. You made such a difference to his happiness. He said you were the son he always wanted, and that he knew you were the only one to continue his legacy." She reached forward and plucked two tissues from the leather-bound box beside Jack. Dabbing her eyes with trembling hands, Miss Karlsson's vulnerability had him wanting to hug her. "Reading of the will won't be until next week, but I wanted you to know now. It's one less concern for you, at least. You'll never have to worry about money again."

"And you, and all the staff, won't have to worry about it either. Not while I'm in charge. I'm going to give large bonuses to everyone. It'll be a gift from Dante, for your faithful service," said Jack.

She nodded, smile mixing with grimace. "That's the sort of generosity we'd expect from

Dante. He picked his heir wisely. Thank you, Jack."

"I thought I'd become a man. Now I feel like a child again, overwhelmed by adult things. I'll need your support for a while to come. I hope you'll give me it." He knew the answer but needed to hear the words.

"Without question. As will everyone else here. They all care about you," she said, smiling with sad eyes.

"I never saw him lose his temper with anyone. Even with me at my most annoying." He was musing, not sure what reply he wanted.

"He had such patience. Especially for you. You brought new purpose to his life and, oh God, before I forget"—she opened the folder on her lap and handed him an envelope— "from Dante. He told me to give you this, should anything happen to him."

Jack's name was written on it in elegant black ink. It reminded him of the night before the painting test, all those years ago.

Leather squeaked as she stood and dropped her crumpled tissues into the wastepaper basket. "I'll leave you to read it in private. The service starts at 1 o' clock, so Harbir will be waiting outside at noon to take us. Is there anything you need?"

He ran his fingertips over the envelope's luxuriant fibre. "No, thanks. I'll be ready before noon. Thank you so much, Miss Karlsson. You're a good friend."

In his earlier teens he'd savoured every opportunity to watch her leave. Now he focused on the envelope in his hands. A final message from the only person he'd ever loved.

Slicing along its top with a silver letter opener, he slid the thick cream paper out and straightened its crisp folds. It read like this:

My beloved Jack,

If you are reading this letter, then my story has ended.

I know it seems unfair, but, unfortunately, our stories end the way they want to, not how we choose. More importantly though, your story is continuing, so remain strong and positive as it unfolds.

It's ok to feel sad. Weep, but do not get lost in depressing thoughts over what cannot be changed. Enjoy your life, explore, adventure. Maybe you will find the answers I could not. Whatever happens, I believe you will triumph over any adversity that comes across your path.

You may be thinking you can solve this situation by painting me. Do not. There is only one Dante De Luca. I refuse to be imitated. I repeat: Do NOT paint me. Ever. My fate is no different from every other soul born into this fleeting chaos we call life. Death happens, regardless of gifts. Accept this and your life will be far happier.

Jack, you were not only the apprentice I was looking for, but the son I wanted. My body may have died, but my love for you is eternal. I will remain alive in your heart.

I wish my ashes to be scattered somewhere beautiful.

You decide the place.

With deepest love,

Dante De Luca

P.s. As you know, there are only three people within the palace who have knowledge of what we are: Harbir, Jaheem and Miss Karlsson. I strongly suggest you do not expand this circle of confidence, unless vital. A secret known by many is not a secret.

Jack re-folded the letter, slid it back inside the envelope, and wept.

❋ ❋ ❋

The crematorium at LochElphin was ill-prepared for Jack and his entourage. Its chair rows packed with palace staff, standing space in the rear and side areas was a case of shuffles and shoulders pressed tight. Attendees were a huddle of gloomy faces and silence save for sporadic tears and sniffles.

Coats, gloves and scarves—all black, brown or dark grey—reflected the biting gusts roaming free around the town's streets. Winding through the glens, clouds had spattered the limo's windows in their spittle. The vehicle's heating hadn't stopped his shivers, but blue skies and sunshine wouldn't have seen him feeling any warmer.

Musty chapel smell—dusty stone, tattered hymn books and damp carpets—made Jack reluctant to breathe through his nose as he eased the knot of his black tie a fraction, mindful of keeping respect. Designer and silk, the damn thing felt like a fancy noose.

The service started with a priest offering words of hollow comfort. Miss Karlsson and Jaheem gave eulogies; hers elegant, his gruff, but both poignant. The crowd sang songs to an invisible god. Jack didn't join in.

All the while he was sobbing; his system clenched in a toxic cocktail of numbness and adrenaline as he stared at the coffin draped in an Italian flag. A life so magnificent, ended without warning in a matter of seconds. It was injustice.

Then came the final moment. The box was lowered, sent on its descent with ghastly pitches of organ music. Then it was gone. Flames from the furnace would already be hissing at the wood.

No. That wasn't going to be Dante's end. They still had more stories together. He'd find a way.

✻ ✻ ✻

The banquet hall had streets of buffet stretched along its sides. Miss Karlsson had brought in catering companies—only the best, of course—so the palace chefs and waiting staff could have time off for Dante's wake. Collective respect had always been paramount in the palace, and rank was not going to be a factor when it came to mourning rights.

Purse strings had been torn off and strewn. Hefty kegs of craft ale and a dazzling spectrum of finest spirits and liqueurs were arranged within pop-up pubs both inside and outside the hall's ornate walls. Legions of wine bottles—red, white and rose—were rarest vintage. Sommeliers in spotless gloves and black bow ties popped corks and poured generous glasses.

Salty teases of spit-roasted venison and beef sidled across tables and up noses. Fresh smoked salmon was sliced and served, ripe red lobsters were cracked and smothered in garlic butter, buns—slid straight from ovens—were dished in dozens from silver tongs, their doughy aromas caressing and comforting nostrils and stomachs.

Lilies, gladioli and roses perfumed; bunched and flared in magnificence wherever space was spare. Grilled spice blended with pollen, grape and hop. Drinks tipped, teeth munched, and tongues chattered as the hall heaved with hugs, sighs and puffy eyes.

But Jack's tastebuds were uninspired, dry. He had appetite for taming fate and little else.

Sitting in the quietest corner, hunched and hoping to avoid eye contact, he was staring at his loafers. Sleek and velvet with bridges badged in silver, their satin lining was snug. They'd cost a lot of money. He looked around at the lake of black suits and dresses and wished every solution was a simple matter of cash. Then he'd have no problems.

"You have unexpected guests."

He looked up to see the colossal frame of his friend—and now personal bodyguard—Jaheem. Everyone was sombre, but an extra edge of concern seemed etched on his broad forehead.

"Tell me it's not who I think it is," asked Jack. He loosened his tie knot further and rubbed tongue against teeth, searching for saliva. He was running on reserves, drained by trauma and frustration.

Jaheem answered with a frown and nod.

"Dammit. Today of all days. Who's with him?"

"That steroid abuser with the gold teeth. And three others. All men of the same ilk." With a hand like bunched bananas, he pressed Jack's shoulder in gentle grip. "If you can't deal with it, it's ok. This is a taxing day for you. I will tell him to come back tomorrow. Or not at all. You are the boss now, not him."

Eight years. He hadn't seen or heard from his da—that person in eight years. Near half his life. "Where are they now?"

"Waiting in the reception hall, no doubt boring Miss Karlsson."

Jack exhaled, the gust petering into sigh. "Ok, I'll see him and Hendy in the Sapphire Lounge. The others can be brought in here but have someone keep an eye on them. And Jaheem"—he stood with reluctance— "please stay close by my side. I'm feeling fragile, mate."

"Of course, don't worry. I'll have security on standby too. Not that I would need their help."

❊ ❊ ❊

The Sapphire Lounge was plush. Intended as a piano bar for evening entertaining, the actual piano—a grand, gleaming black one—hadn't been played in years. Dante's lukewarm attitude to parties meant the instrument had become a mere ornament with musical options.

Jack's uninvited guests were sat on the central sofa. Arthur sipping espresso and Hendy swilling cognac, two seat cushions apart. The years had been lenient on them. Arthur's forehead was craggier, and the slick of his hair smattered with grey, but he hadn't shrivelled into bone and wrinkles. Hendy's jacket arms were still stuffed with muscle, though the gym regimen had slackened, judging from his waistline. Both wore tailored suits, shiny shoes and flashy watches. Jack's money contributing towards costs, no doubt.

Jack was reclining in a wingback armchair, shifting against its smooth cushioning in vain search of comfort. There was nothing wrong with the chair.

He'd already been sitting when they'd entered. Arthur had extended open arms but been given a cool greeting and invited to sit instead. The bartender had brought drinks while Hendy flashed toothy smiles and Arthur's eyes roamed the room.

Jack was taking regular gulps of icy orange juice to soothe his parched throat and warm forehead. Jaheem was standing beside his chair with tree branch arms folded. Seven and a half feet of sinewy warning.

Arthur's espresso cup clinked out bitter vapours as he rested it on its saucer. "So, here we all are, on this sad day, after so many years apart." Looking at Jaheem he nodded with a thin smile, saying softly, "Hello again, big fella. Forgotten your name. Jabbar or something, wasn't it? Anyway"—he leaned forward, resting elbows on thighs, his dark green paisley tie dangling—"look at you, son. All grown up. Too good to hug your old man now, eh?"

"It's been eight years. I didn't think you were desperate for hugs?" Jack took another mouthful of juice. The frosty zest was cooling, calming. He placed the glass back down and tried to keep his deep breathing discreet.

Arthur's mouth closed, the skin along his jawline twitching. Then, with a nod and strained smile, he replied, "It's ok, I understand, son. Eight years is a long time, and you're grieving your, uh, teacher. But it was what he wanted. I read between the lines of his terms. He didn't want me causing distractions. You should be thanking me."

"He's right. Wasn't easy for your dad, not seeing you, Jack. Believe me," Hendy said in husky agreement before slurping from his cognac. He wouldn't be getting a refill.

Jack took a deep breath. His lips were quivering. "Ok then, thank you. Now what do you want? Did you come to give me my money?" It was peanuts to him now, but he was hopeful the question would cause discomfort.

Pink surged in Arthur's lumpy cheeks. "Well, that was another thing the old geez—Mr De Luca said, wasn't it? To be careful giving substantial amounts like that, to young men like you. You might do yourself an injury with it, eh? But don't worry, it's safe. Been investing it for you. It'll be yours all in good time, after you come home."

"I am home." His tie was tight again. He clutched the chair with clammy palms and shifted hip position.

"Come on son, your teacher—God rest his soul—is dead. Passed on. He isn't coming back. This place ain't your home no more. Your apprenticeship's over. You'll be getting kicked out soon enough. Come back down to London. I've got a swanky new house in Kensington. Seven bedrooms, you can take your pick. I'll set you up in a nice little studio for doing your paintings. You make the product and I'll take care of the marketing and sales. Fifty-fifty, father and son. What do you say?"

"I say, this is my home and I have my own studio here. A huge one. And I won't be getting kicked out of my own property, ever," said Jack, allowing himself smug indulgence as he spoke.

"What, you mean—"

"Is this place—"

"Put a sock in it, will ya?" Arthur snapped with a raised palm at Hendy, before glaring at

Jack with peeled eyes. "You mean that soft old git left you all this? You must be joking. Did he go bloody senile? Are you saying this place is yours now?" The questions were barrelling from his mouth amongst flecks of coffee-tinged spit.

Jack had heard enough. He pointed to the door. "He was more of a father than you ever were. And I had to see him lying in a coffin today. If you can't speak with respect, then you should leave. Keep the money you owe me. As severance pay." Pressing palms against the chair's arms, sweat was seeping onto the fabric, causing damp friction against his skin.

"You what?"

"Keep the money. I want nothing from you, ever again. Jaheem"—he blew out a shaky exhale — "our guests are leaving. Make sure they get to their car safely." Shivering, his forehead was radiating heat and he wanted the bathroom.

Hendy necked the remaining cognac, clunked the glass down and stood. Arthur did the same, with cheeks pulsing red as roses. Neither of them motioned to leave. Around six feet of Persian carpet lay between Jack and his—now officially estranged—father. Hendy smirked in silence. Arthur scowled and goaded.

"You man enough to make me leave yourself then? Or you gonna hide behind your gorilla?"

Jack's mouth had turned to sandpaper. Neck quaking and tongue trembling, he said, "Jaheem show the gentlemen out. By any means necessary."

"Ha thought so. All mouth. Just like his mum. Not got the balls, do ya, Little Picasso?"

The words slapped at his stomach. He wanted to do something, but his limbs—taut with capable muscle—were heavy, like magnets were holding them to the chair. Neither fists nor words would form. He was paralysed.

Jaheem intervened. Unfolding his massive arms, he pointed to the door. "You can leave by the door. Or"—he nodded to the tall windowpanes— "the window. Choose." They were on the second floor.

Fists clenched; Hendy took a step forward. Arthur held out his palm in a stop motion, before shrugging and fastening the two buttons on his suit jacket. "If that's what you want, but"—he wagged his finger at Jack— "I'm still your father, whether you like it or not. You uppity little shit."

Leaving at a grudging pace, they walked towards the door with Jaheem shadowing them. "Disappointed in you, Jack, talking to your dad like that. Expected better from you," said Hendy over his shoulder.

"I'll see you around, son." Arthur stopped at the door, straightened his tie and glowered up at Jaheem. "And you, you want to be careful how you talk to people. You're not bulletproof."

Arthur and his crew left. The wake continued. Jack went straight to bed, sick from stress.

CHAPTER 19

Giddy, he stumbled onto his backside with legs sprawling on rigid wood. His clothes' chaotic paint spatter matched the studio floorboards. Panting, shaking, he gazed in amazement at what he'd done.

Engulfed, swallowed; Jack's emotions were still spinning, churning, rising and falling; chaotic, colliding, like flailing flakes in a shaken snow globe. He'd formed his creation on the biggest stretched canvas the studio ceilings and doors could accommodate.

It was a masterpiece unrivalled on earth.

It had been weeks since Dante's funeral. Mission clear and heart ablaze, Jack's passion had raged daily, rampaging; his strokes defiant, bold, unyielding as they gifted life, eternity and hope in abundance of brushed colour and jealous love.

Swelling, spilling, his eyes streaming and heart heaving; he'd screamed and cursed—trying to purge the grief of his loss—but there had been no quench for his savage thirst.

No longer flesh and bone, his fingers had become extensions of the wooden tools he wielded. He'd breathed nothing but texture, contours, colour and tone. Time had been smacked from his mind, kicked out and the studio door closed behind as he'd carved a world in paint and desperate wishes free of restraint. Now it was finished, the canvas' texture gleamed and crackled with unique vibrancy.

Sitting amongst pots, brushes and palettes was the urn for Dante's ashes. Empty.

Justice would be done. Dante would live once more.

* * *

Bubble wrap in thick layers and palace staff taking great care saw the masterpiece moved to the Gallery of Galleries. Now it hung there, framed in ornate gold. Real gold.

Emeralds, sapphires, diamonds; the fields, rivers and snowy mountain tops sparkled like gemstones. Jack had created a land of bounty and variety. Every rich and wondrous geographical feature imaginable was contained within its boundaries, except desert. Dante wasn't overly keen on desert.

Individual people weren't portrayed, but the swathes of hamlets, villages and towns would be abuzz with healthy, contented residents. A world of wonderful people for Dante to discover. Jack had wished it so. Even a recluse like Dante would find close friends, within the timescale of eternity.

Miss Karlsson and Harbir stared with peeled eyes and open mouths. Thousands of the world's finest artworks hung above and around them, but their attention was channelled straight ahead.

"I've nev—the mountain peaks"—Miss Karlsson's heels sang out brief clacks as she stepped close to peer— "they're glinting. And the rivers, I—I can hear the water moving. How? The flowers, the trees. I can smell them. Bitter cedar. Sweet roses. Too many to count. How on earth? Not even Dante painted something so alive. It's incredible. It's—"

"The greatest masterpiece in all history," said Harbir. Eyes distant and voice loud, he announced as if to an imaginary audience. Walking to beside Miss Karlsson, his face roamed the rolling landscape in its pristine glory. "You've outdone yourself, Jack. Dante would be so proud."

"Why does it appear electrified?" Jaheem's tone was cautious, missing the joy detectable from his companions. "And that huge castle on the hill. My eyes are drawn to it every time, like a magnet. No matter where I look, I find myself gravitating towards it."

Harbir nodded. "Mine too. It's like the place is familiar."

"Yes, yes. That familiarity. I feel it as well," said Miss Karlsson. "And I'd also like to know why on earth it's doing that? As Jaheem says, it's like some sort of electricity."

Tiny blue crackles were wisping across the canvas in erratic waves. He'd checked for any danger before letting the palace team carry the painting. The currents were harmless but gave Jack extra hope about the wonders awaiting within.

"I can't tell you the exact reason why it's like that, as—being completely honest with you—I don't know. I think it's because of the unique composition of this painting." Jack took three strides with hands on hips, before turning to face his friends again. "But I can tell you about my masterpiece in more detail and let you draw your own conclusions." He pointed to the grand castle. "Easy part first: that's the focal point on the canvas, and I made it intentionally so. The name of it is Castello di Dante, also known as Dante's Castle. He's the owner. He's in there right now, enjoying the luxury we all know he likes. I—"

"What? Dante is in—"

"Please, Miss Karlsson, with respect, let me finish or we'll be here all night. And"—Jack nodded to the leather satchel near his feet – "I have an important journey to make. Now, as I said, Dante is in there. I didn't make him a king or a lord or whatever because I know he's too modest for titles. But he's in there. I know it. I wished it so hard so many times as my brush touched the canvas, it almost cost me my sanity."

The place was silent, except for creaks from Jaheem's bulky leather boots.

"So, to clarify, I was given two final instructions from Dante. The first one was that I should never paint him under any circumstances. I obeyed. He told me to scatter his ashes somewhere beautiful, in a place of my choice. I obeyed."

Jack gestured to the shimmering masterpiece with open palms. A crackle pulsed across the castle as he raised his voice, saying, "I took his mortal remains and made them immortal. I didn't paint him but painted *with* him, to make his own world. This world."

Harbir raised an index and asked at the same time. "Ah, Jack. You're saying the masterpiece and the world it contains is...made from Dante?"

"Yes. It is Il Mundo di Dante"—he paused, smiling at the painting— "also known as Dante's World."

* * *

Hanging the broad shoulder strap across his chest, and adjusting it to a snug fit, Jack stood with the leather satchel nestled comfortably under his arm. He'd made sure it held a complete range of brushes, paints and other tools. It was unlikely any in-world painting would be necessary, but once he reached the castle, he'd gift it to Dante. No doubt he'd want to add his own signature to aspects of the world Jack had made. And paint ice-cold pina coladas.

Dressed in a thin cashmere crew neck, skinny jeans and chic trainers, he was expecting pleasant weather—he'd wished for it in the green lowlands where the castle sat—but if any breezes breathed a little too cool, he could always paint himself a jacket. Journeys inside Dante's World were going to be easy, in any case.

"Jack, I don't know about this." Jaheem—in his usual stance, cross-armed like a colossus chiselled from onyx—was still staring at the masterpiece with narrowed eyelids. "Are you sure you want to go in there?"

He rolled his eyes. "Are you joking? Not even

you could stop me. That's how badly I want to get in there. Look, mate, I know what I'm doing. I'm going to see Dante again. My father. My *real* father. Why are you looking so worried?"

"We don't know what effect his ashes have had on the world beneath. And"—he turned his eyes to the two others as if appealing— "at times, you spent days on end in the studio with little sleep, little food. I worry you weren't in the right frame of mind the whole time."

The padded shoulders of Harbir's stylish navy suit rose a fraction as he shrugged. "That I didn't see"—he nodded at Il Mundo di Dante—"all I know is what I can see now. A world of serenity and harmony. Even the currents are hypnotic, calming. I can't see any problem at all. Miss Karlsson, your thoughts?"

Her citrusy perfume was in competition with the painting's fragrances. She was finger-combing her shiny blonde fringe, inspecting Il Mundo di Dante. "I was a little worried about you at times if I'm being honest. Dante told me emotions are crucial when it comes to painting. Would you say yours were stable the whole time you painted this? You didn't seem yourself. I think there was—understandably—an outpouring of grief. You don't feel that might be a problem?"

"Relax. My overwhelming passion created positivity." Jack was speaking in half-truths. His passion had created positivity. At times. At other times, he'd simply been overwhelmed. It didn't matter though. Dante's essence flowed across the canvas. The world under it would be wonderful. "Anyway, my mind's made up. I'm going in. What messages would you like me to pass on to Dante?"

Miss Karlsson let out a sigh from her smile. "Just tell him we miss him." She met the eyes of the others. "I think that's at least one thing we can all agree on, yes?"

"Yes, most definitely. Please tell him if only we could enter through the canvas, we would be there too," said Harbir with a firm reply.

Frowning, Jaheem exhaled through his nose and nodded. "Same. And I wish I could come with you. To keep you safe if nothing else."

He clasped a reassuring palm on Jaheem's arm. The muscle was like marble and thicker than Jack's thigh. "Safe? Mate"—he pointed to his masterpiece— "I'm the creator of that, and I made it with the help of the greatest painter who ever lived. Nothing's going to hurt me. Besides"—patting the satchel at his side, he smiled— "I'm armed and dangerous. What could possibly go wrong?"

With that, he stepped through the canvas, met by bright light and the world beyond.

CHAPTER 20

That was something new. He'd emerged waist deep among the portal's fizzing rays and had to push himself up and out, using the grassy banks around him.

In all the paintings he'd visited, portals were always suspended in the air. But then, this was no ordinary world, so it made sense the entrance would be extraordinary.

Now he was surrounded by cedar. They'd come up wonderfully. Standing with hands on hips, he tilted his upper body backwards to appreciate the trees' full glory. Their chunky trunks soared; the robust branches draped in nature's luxuriance. Pine needles and cones combined to make zesty perfume. Jack breathed in the fresh scents and strode across grass, enjoying its lush carpet brushing against his trainers. Warm sunshine dripped in patches between gaps in the canopy, dappling the healthy emerald path as birds—joyous in their melodies—serenaded from on high. What a glorious forest. By far his best example.

On he went, in search of Castello di Dante and its chief occupant, with a hopeful soul and smile. His strides took him past gurgling streams and clearings bathed in rays, thriving with daisies and dandelions. Squirrels scampered, frogs hopped and croaked, and in the distance, he saw glimpses of deer, munching on shrubbery with gentle bends of their elegant necks.

Jack considered jogging but was delighting too much in the details of Il Mundo di Dante. He wondered how much his handiwork had been bolstered by Dante's creative essence. The place was brimming with harmony.

The forest stretched for pleasant miles, until he reached a path around twelve feet wide. Rustic, the stones forming it were clean, smooth and cobbled randomly.

He continued his journey. Excited but also apprehensive, he hoped Dante wouldn't be too angry at finding himself part of a painting. Jack *had* obeyed him—technically—in every respect. And he'd given Dante the most amazing place to enjoy and explore. A world that was at one with Dante, made from his own being. He'd see the sense in it once they were reunited as father and son.

Sunshine flitted in shining bursts between clouds broad and puffy. It was fine, but he'd expected more azure than white. The road was long, with rich waves of wheat swaying either side. Light sweat formed underneath his fringe, kissed cool by breeze. He was enjoying a pace which gave his cardio system an exertion it hadn't had for weeks.

Using his hand as a visor, he scanned the horizon. There it was. His destination sat on a magnificent hill. Dante's Castle. It announced majesty, even at that distance. The home of a legend, a hero.

The path meandered down a hill and then continued in twists and winds. Wheat was replaced with sweeping meadows. Trees and shrubbery lined the route, including rose bushes badged in multi-colour. Red, pink and yellow were pretty but what compelled Jack to stop and marvel were the fourth type: bright royal blue. Their heads' layered elegance reminded him of Harbir's turbans. Jack took hold of one and pinched its fleshy petals between his fingers. Smooth as suede. He stooped and tickled the tip of his nose against the folds. It smelled of drizzled honey, robust with earthy sweetness.

The thorns though. They looked like oversized scorpion stings. Thorns were, naturally, part of a rose, but he did wonder if these ones had to be quite so sharp. Perhaps that was the barb that went with such freakish beauty. He made a mental note to ask Dante about it.

"Good afternoon, lovely day, isn't it?" chirped a female voice from behind.

Gasping, he released the rose with a flinch, turning to be met by two fellow pedestrians. They were a girl and man who looked to be father and daughter. She was about the same age as Jack. At least, no older than twenty. Milk-skinned and slender, she was dressed in a long flowing skirt and white blouse under a green bodice, tied in the centre with leather laces. They were under strain.

Not a problem for Jack. Her health was—quite evidently—no cause for concern. The man's was a different picture, however.

He was using a crutch. Scuffed and scratched, its wooden frame was taking pressure off a withered leg. That was a problem. He didn't expect everyone in Dante's World to be at the exact same stage of youthful bloom, but people were all supposed to be healthy and happy.

"Sorry, young sir. Hope we didn't give you a fright? We would have walked right past, except your clothing is so unusual, my daughter was desperate to say hello," said the man with a farmer-like accent and smile bunched in stubble. His clothes were of the same era as the girl's: several hundred years back from modern fashion.

"Father, please. You make me sound like a nymph. Desperate to say hello, indeed. I just wondered about his costume, is all," said the girl with tongue tutting and eyelids fluttering, blush ripening her pale cheeks. Her bodice seemed to be inflating, as if subtly thrust in his direction.

"Don't worry, miss. There's no misunderstanding. And yes, sir, my clothes are unusual, it's true. I'm, erm, going to a fancy-dress party, at a friend's house. This was my attempt to look different."

The man croaked a chuckle. "You certainly succeeded. Look at those shoes, never seen anything like them."

"Well, you look wonderful, in any case." The girl was trying to sound aloof. Her eyes both shied away and flashed in mischief. "You must be so clever to come up with an outfit like that. I'm Mary, by the way. Pleased to meet you."

She was gorgeous—he'd done fine work there—but Jack couldn't let her poor dad hobble his way through Dante's World. He'd help now while he had the chance. "Thank you, Mary. Me too. Oh, and I'm Jack. But"—he focused on the man— "I hope you won't find it rude. May I ask what happened to your leg?"

The man shrugged his free shoulder. "Not much to say, really. Just been like this forever. Nothing to be done about it. It's not so bad though"—he looked at Mary with a smile— "my beloved daughter takes care of me. Don't you, love?"

Mary stared at Jack, simpering and nodding.

"Well, I am a naturally caring person, so people say…"

"I don't doubt it," said Jack before nodding at his satchel and tapping one of its shiny buckles. "I have some ointments in here that will help your leg. I mean really help it. They can heal you, actually."

The man jerked his neck a fraction and grinned. "Ointments? Meaning no offence, but I don't think there's any ointment can heal this. A bloody miracle might, but not much else."

"Father!"

"Sorry, love. I do apologize, young sir."

Jack waved his hand in dismissal. "Why don't you humour me? I promise its safe, and free of charge. All I want to do is help. It'll only take a few minutes."

Mary persuaded her father, Thomas, to sit on the grass and let Jack treat his leg.

Unbuckling his satchel, he took out the bamboo box inside, laid it on the ground and opened the lid with a click of its brass button. Aside from tiny speckles of dust, Thomas' trousers, which were puffy to knee level then tapered to his ankle, were jet black. Easy peasy. Jack wouldn't even have to remove the cloth or do any mixing.

Opening a pot of black, he dipped the largest brush, bringing it out with the bristles coated. Jack took gentle hold of Thomas' ankle and began long brushstrokes up and down the length of his scrawny limb.

Mary's voice was whispered as she watched. "What kind of ointment goes right on the clothing? And why are you using a paintbrush? Surely it ca—"

The leg began to bulge within its woollen covering as Jack silently wished for the paint to create strong bones and supple muscle, bound with healthy ligaments, tendons and veins, all in perfect ratio to Thomas' physique.

It took a matter of minutes. The paint had worked well. Jack looked up to see Thomas' mouth and eyes wide. "You won't need your crutch ever ag—"

"My God, lad! It's a bloody miracle!" Thomas leapt to his feet, hugging Jack with such force they stumbled on a clump of grass and almost toppled. "That's not ointment, that's bloody magic, I say!"

After teary laughter, tight hugs and smothering cheek pecks from Mary—pleasant ones, Jack admitted—father and daughter were on their way with excited chatter, striding and skipping in the warm sunshine, turning every few minutes to wave and shout loud thanks as they did so.

Jack had made them promise to keep his actions confidential, but the level of their elation said that was unlikely. Anyway, the main thing was he'd changed lives for the better. And he wouldn't make a habit of public painting. It would be for emergencies only.

One thing was clear: his masterpiece was flawed. How deeply remained to be seen.

He decided on a fast jog to Dante's Castle.

CHAPTER 21

The towns and villages were nice. The people were nice. The weather was nice.

Nice wasn't enough. It was supposed to be wonderful. As things stood, Dante's World was little different than the real one, except—judging from the technology and clothes—at least four or five hundred years in the past. Jack had painted traditional buildings with modernity in mind. That hadn't materialised.

Jogging through communities, over cobbled streets, past inns, cottages, farms and windmills, he'd seen youth, smiles, health and happiness. Fringed with sickness and frailty. The flaws ran deep. He hoped Dante was unaffected.

Now stood at the base of the castle's steep hill, he looked up, puffing heavily. His sweater was sticking, especially on the satchel side. The leather bag had grown heavier with each mile. Jack was fit, but he must have run two marathons. He walked, giving his burning lungs a chance to calm, pulling his sweater in and out with wafting motions as he went.

The path wound upwards, lined with cherry blossoms on either side. Their branches arched high, intwining into a lattice of fluffy clumps. Floral confetti smattered the ground in scatters as robust gusts ruffled pink puffs above.

After about ten minutes his breathing had steadied, and the cashmere was less clingy. Trees on one side gave way to the castle's lofty walls and bulky ramparts. He had to crane his head far back to see their tops. It was as massive as he'd depicted it on canvas, though the fortifications were enhanced, chunkier. How pointless, with no enemy to defend against.

Still not fully recovered from the impromptu cross-country running, he walked with all the speed he could muster, keen to meet Dante and confirm his father and friend was unaffected by the imperfections Jack had—obviously—transmitted onto the canvas.

The broad cobbles continued straight until he came to a smaller path branching from them. Worn grass and narrow, it stretched to a small lake. He could see part of its rippling surface peeking from between trees and bushes. A cooling swim would have been perfect if he hadn't—

They can't touch the stars like me.
No, not like me
In my dreams.
Yes, in my dreams.

Someone was singing by the lake. Feminine melodies floated towards him, twirling amongst leaves and breeze.

The branches dance in the breeze
But bound by roots is every tree.
They can't wander free like me.
No, not like me
In my dreams.
Yes, in my dreams.

The bright tones sent his scalp tingling, buzzes pulsing down his neck. Jack needed to see who she was. Just for a minute. Heavenly lyrics guided him along the grass path. He reached the lakeside but saw nobody.

The lioness hunts where she wants
But bound by mountains and the sea.
She can never roam like me.
No, not like me
In my dreams.
Yes, in my dreams.

The exquisite chimes were coming from behind a thicket of red and blue rose bushes near the lake's edge. Jack stepped towards it with his pricey trainers sinking into wet mocha sand. Not wanting to cause startlement, he crouched, peering through a gap between petals and thorns.

Wow. He was met with an unexpected view. A lady with a stunning figure. And no clothes on. He could only see her lower back, from just above hips down to knees, where they met with the wind-kissed surface she was wading in. His eyes lingered on her porcelain skin before he tore them away. One of Dante's teachings leapt to mind: *A painter must always be a gentleman even if his instincts would have him not be.*

He wouldn't look, but he could take a moment to enjoy the enchantment of her ballad before pressing on to Dante. Quietly moving to behind a nearby boulder, he peeled off the satchel's leather strap—it was still damp from sweat—and sat on a patch of daisy-speckled grass, resting his back on smooth stone.

The Titans peak in the sky
But bound by—

Song rocketed to shriek. Jack bolted upright, jolted by ear-juddering pitch. There were heavy sploshes across the water. Multiple people, moving in hurried lunges.

Then men's voices. Breathing hard, aggressive. "You're coming with us, wolf girl."

"Shit, she's even uglier than people say."

"Help! Help!"

"Shut your mouth, you monster, or I'll gut you." Jack heard the sing of steel being pulled from a scabbard. "You see this? You're coming with us."

"Don't you dare touch me! Help! Somebody please help me!"

Curses and screams mashed with splashes.

Jack fumbled at the satchel's buckles, pulling the bamboo box out and onto the ground with a clatter. Clicking it open with shaking hands, he dipped a large brush in the first paint pot he could get hold of. His body thumping from blood flow, he raced round the thicket into ankle-deep water.

Splayed on the ground, the victim was clinging to modesty with a soaked linen undergarment clutched across her front. Lashing out with pink-soled feet, she squealed and shrieked at two assailants grasping at her limbs. The third attacker—a broad-shouldered man in tattered leather armour—was standing with sword in hand, shouting threats. "Stop kicking or I'll chop your feet off!"

But that wasn't the scene's most shocking aspect. The woman was a—she had the head of a wolf! What on earth—

"Who the bloody hell are you?" Jack's sudden entrance had alerted the swordman, who was now facing him. He scowled with the blade raised high, poised to strike. "I said who the bloody hell are you?"

Jack held the brush's wooden handle in tight clasp at his side, realizing he'd never actually considered how to use one as a weapon. "Let the —let the lady go. You don't want to mess with me, mate."

The thug lowered the sword's tip and made two rapid flicks in a directing motion towards the path. "Piss off, jester. This isn't your business. Turn around and go back where you came from. Go on, move, while you're still breathing."

The other two now had hold of the wolf woman's shoulders and were trying to drag her onto feet. "Help, please!" Her wide, wailing mouth was full of jagged white teeth. One solid clamp and twist from those jaws would have seen fingers floating in the lake. But she wasn't using them. Why the hell not?

Jack's trainers were planted in the cold shallows. He gripped the paintbrush, knowing it's—obvious—power, but he'd never even had a fist fight before. He opened his mouth, but nothing came out.

"Right, that's it, come here you simple bastard." The armed man stomped forward with a face contorted in fury. His sword gleamed like a giant steak knife.

Jack didn't want to be the fillet. Letting out a gasp, he stumbled backwards. The tip of his brush erupted in spits and pops of energy, its paint crackling in bright blue potency.

The attacker roared, swinging in a sideways hacking motion. Jack held up his arm in defence. Blade and bristles collided.

A blast thundered from the brush. Smoke belched as forceful roar hammered the thug backwards into his companions, leaving all three would-be kidnappers strewn flat, splashing, spluttering and wheezing. Torrents of putrid fumes—stinking like rotten eggs—were streaming from the fizzing bristles like a distress flare. Jack's eyes were stinging, welling with liquid as he heard one of the gang members gasp between violent coughs, "He's a wizard. Come on. Go!"

Faces blackened and hair burnt, they limped off, leaving their sword and eyebrows lying by the lakeside.

The wolf woman, also coughing but appearing unhurt, crawled further up the bank, towards clothing folded on the grass in a pile. From a kneeling position she began hurriedly unfolding the clothes.

Wafting away the last black wisps, Jack wiped his eyes and stared. A woman with a wolf's head. Or was it a wolf with a woman's body? Either way, something had gone seriously wrong with his masterpiece.

Holding the folds of an emerald and gold silk dress against her body she turned with amber eyes and broad snout focused.

"Miss, are you—"

"Don't stand there gawking at me. I'm the Princess Oakenfol, not a tavern wench. Turn your back. Go on, turn around, you bloody pervert."

"Of course, sorry, erm, princess."

Princess Oakenfol? Jack hadn't wished royalty into Dante's World. He needed to get into that castle straight away.

CHAPTER 22

Precise granite flagstones lined the edges of trimmed grass peppered in peach trees and blackberry bushes. Leaves rustled on branches swaying in supple bends, fat with velvet fruit. Blackberries hung swollen on vines; their segments clumped in shiny goodness. The small orchard offered freshly picked succulence.

There was an artificial stream meandering through the centre; its gurgling currents boasting fish bright-scaled and well-fed. In the far corner sat a waist-high marble plinth with two large terracotta jugs and half a dozen steel goblets arranged alongside. One had water, the other red wine. Jack had already guzzled four cups of the former, reviving his struggling tongue and throat with cooling gulps.

Yes, the quadrangle he'd been told to wait in

—gruffly, by a chainmail-clad guard—was a garden of delights. An impressive oasis, indeed.

One he wasn't in the mood to appreciate. He didn't care about fruit, fish or vintage. He needed to know about Dante. Was he in the castle or not? Was he even in this world? If so—after the relief of reunion—he and Dante would work out solutions for the masterpiece. If not, Jack would go back to the portal at once and never return. He would move the painting along its tracks to the quietest corner of the Gallery of Galleries and seal the canvas permanently with plexi-glass, or, even better, locked metal shutters.

Jack waited, passing a little time by using dry brushes to suck the moisture from his clothes. His impatience growing, he thought of storming through the castle to look for Dante, but he had no clue where that might be. If anywhere. And he didn't fancy setting off more brush bombs if the armed guards objected to his exploration. No, he'd wait.

Rays shaded in apricot, rose and magenta filtered through wide stone arches looking over the vast castle complex below. Beyond that, the sun eased its way downwards, under the horizon. Stunning. Stars speckled. Sparse at first, then coating the night sky in their sparkles.

A young boy made the rounds, lighting wall torches. Jack plucked a puckle of blackberries and a peach, poured more water, and sat on the broad ledge of an arch, gazing up at his celestial handiwork. At least he'd done that right.

The same stocky guard returned. His scowl and tone had softened. "Follow me, please."

"About time," muttered Jack as he wiped palms on jeans—the fruit had been dripping with sweet juice—and stood, slinging the satchel strap over his shoulder and following the soldier, whose chainmail chinked in silvery whispers as he walked.

The man led him across broad courtyards and through lengthy corridors, guarded at intervals by sentinels armoured in steel plate and clasping heavy looking spears. They eventually reached a pair of tall wooden doors, reinforced with thick iron bars stretched across their planks.

There were two guards on duty. Receiving a nod from the man in chainmail, they gave a quick "sir" and opened the doors, stepping to the side in clinks and clanks.

They entered a grand hall. Bare flagstone became carpet. Luxuriantly woven, its crimson fibres were spongy under his trainer treads. Light flowed and flickered from huge candelabra both hanging from the ceiling and perched on wrought iron stands placed around the room. Tapestries, silken banners and stained glass told Jack this was a court of some kind.

If that hadn't, the man sitting on the enormous throne would have.

He—whoever he was—was sat atop a flight

of chunky stone steps. The throne's high back was upholstered in what looked like lion skin, with a mane running along the top edge, while the arms were draped with unmistakable spots of leopard leather.

Approaching closer, Jack saw the noble himself was clothed in an elegant maroon doublet, which looked like finest silk, joined in the middle with a line of silver clasps—he only had one arm. His right sleeve was neatly folded and pinned a few inches below the shoulder. Yet more evidence of Jack's defective work.

With knee bent and hand outstretched, Jack's escort announced the mystery ruler's identity. "His Grace, Archduke Cedric Oakenfol."

Fine, but he wasn't Dante. Hope was fading. Jack had screwed up royally. More than the majestic archduke could ever aspire to.

"Your Grace, the, uh, gentleman who—"

"The hero of the story, yes." Voice gravelly but words clear, he stroked his patchy blonde beard, smiling at Jack. "Fought off three brigands who would have kidnapped my daughter. Most impressive. Your name, young man?"

"Jack, sir."

The soldier in chainmail was glaring at Jack through strained eyeballs. "Your Grace, and you should kneel when you approach the archduke." His jaw muscles were tensed, twitching in grimace.

The archduke raised a lazy palm—his only

one, of course—and said, "That's quite alright, Magnus. This young man is an honoured guest." Leaning forward and peering, his lips crimped into a wry smile. "How did a young pup like you fight off three armed men and come out unscathed?"

"Only one was armed, sir. With a sword. Perhaps he wasn't very skilled with it."

He snorted in amusement. "I see. Perhaps. So"—he nodded his thinning dandelion locks at Jack's satchel— "do you keep daggers in that knapsack of yours? A mace? What did you fight them off with? You don't look much of a bare-knuckle fighter to me."

Magnus interrupted through throat clearance. "Beg your pardon, Your Grace, we checked him for weapons before allowing him entry, its only painting tools."

"How curious. A painter, eh? That explains your outfit then. Some of kind of artistic statement, no doubt. So, do tell me, what happened, exactly? Annabelle says you simply chased them off?"

Fumes of burning incense rose from an ornate plinth in the far corner, puffing sweet, woody smoke into the air in snaking wisps. Jack disliked anything that reminded him of Dante's cursed cigars.

"Annabelle?"

The archduke tutted but his smile stayed empathetic. "My daughter, the Princess Oakenfol."

"Oh, the wol—the woman. The lady, I mean. Well, the la—the princess, is too kind. I just startled them, then they ran off because of all the noise I was making. It was no heroism at all, really."

"Nonsense, we are in your debt. You must be rewarded. I will grant you one favour. Name it and—if it is within my power—it shall be done."

There was only one way he might have been able to help. It was worth a try. "I'm looking for a man. His name is Dante. Dante De Luca." Jack paused to check for any glimmer of recognition from the archduke, as well as turning to gauge reaction from the man to his side. Blank faces in both cases.

Magnus shrugged, looking towards the throne. "I'm afraid the name is unknown to me, Your Grace."

"Sorry to say we haven't heard of the gentleman. What I can do, however, is ask someone far more knowledgeable in these matters. Magnus here will take note of your fellow's name and give it to my man, Berenza. If this Dante De Luca can be found, he will be found, I assure you."

The archduke's confidence was nudging hope to stay awake. "Thank you so much, sir. I don't want to appear rude, but do you have any idea how long that might take? If he is to be found, I mean."

"Berenza works quickly when it comes to

finding people. Although he has very recently been set the task of tracking down those scoundrels who accosted my daughter. So, bearing that in mind, he should have an answer—one way or the other—within one or two days. Three at most, I should imagine."

"Well, ok, it's worth a—"

"One thing though. May I ask why you seek this man, this Dante fellow?"

"He's my fa—friend. My close friend, in fact." Jack realised looking for your own father in such an old-fashioned culture might have seemed odd. Most people probably lived within a 1-mile radius of all family, immediate or extended.

"Fine. Magnus, make it clear to Berenza"—he wagged his index twice like a headmaster—"that, should he locate Dante De Luca, he is being sought as a friend and should be treated as such."

"Of course, Your Grace. A friend," replied Magnus. With that, he bowed and left, armour jingling in soft metallic chimes as he went.

The archduke stood. Middle-aged but minimally wrinkled, he was tall at around 6'4, with broad shoulders and a tapered waist. Jack supposed he would have been a formidable warrior if not for his missing arm.

He walked down the steps; his knee-length suede boots silent on the grey stone. Placing a firm palm on Jack's shoulder, he smiled with sky blue eyes. "Now, Jack. What say you to a hearty meal? I think you've earned it."

CHAPTER 23

"I do hope you'll forgive me. Please say you will."

"There's really nothing to forgive. You'd just been attacked, for God's sake. It's completely understandable. Anyone would be upset after that."

"I know, but still. I was ever so rude to you. And after you being so incredibly brave and saving me from those horrible rogues. Please say you'll forgive me, Jack."

He was sitting in a banquet hall, having eaten roasted meats and vegetables, fresh bread and grilled fish. The castle chefs were skilled, and their dishes delivered in relentless courses. Jack wanted to swap his dining chair for a sofa.

As he talked with the Princess Oakenfol, or Annabelle as she now insisted on being called, he scrutinized her appearance, trying to be discreet.

Dressed in a satin gown of lilac and silver with sleeves flared in oversized frills, she was feminine in body and behaviour. Polite, gracious, she blended bashful with a smattering of mischief. A charming lady.

With a wolf's head. Not simply wolf-like, like joined-up eyebrows combined with a severe facial hair problem, but unequivocal wolf: eyes, ears, snout, and fur—the colour of soot-sprinkled hazelnuts—which ended just above her collarbone.

How bizarre. Had corrupted versions of Dante's memories somehow seeped into the canvas and beyond? Had Jack's volatile emotions translated into bedlam? Or both? Perhaps he would never know the truth of the trouble in Dante's World. Or whatever the place was.

And the teeth. Fangs designed for tearing flesh, but she'd chewed on fruit and nibbled cheese during the meal. The archduke had poked fun, voicing his long-standing disagreement with her meat-free diet. She'd replied that killing animals was cruel when there were so many other nutritious foods to be found within nature. A veggie wolf. Really?

"If it makes you feel better then, of course, I forgive you."

"Wonderful. Thank you. So, we're friends then?" she asked, leaning closer with white whiskers twitching. Lavender wafts signalled her liberal approach to applying perfume.

"I don't see why not."

"Well, that makes me incredibly happy. Thank you, Jack. And"—she looked over at her father, who was stood further down the hall, in hushed discussion with an impeccably groomed man in a cream linen cloak— "I didn't mention to anyone about your—you know—with the paintbrushes. I thought it wise to leave that detail out. And of course, I hope in return you won't tell anyone of my"—her furry ears curled a little as she looked to the side, fingertips grazing back and forth along her pearl necklace— "immodesty in front of you."

"Oh, really, please don't feel bad about—"

"You must have seen everything, I suppose. Absolutely everything..." Snout quivering, her jaws parted a fraction. Still looking away, she held one of the white pearls between slender digits, turning it in tender twists. The stark contrast between her manicured fingernails—coated in meticulously applied pink varnish—and furry face was mildly freaking Jack out. He glanced at the satchel beside him. The tools were all there and he wanted to help, but was there even a polite way to offer to fix someone's face?

"No, not at all. I didn't see anything I shouldn't. And I'm sorry for causing any offence. It really was just a glance, to check you were ok."

She let go of her necklace. "Well, good. Yes, good. I'm so glad. And you're such a gentleman, Jack. Thank you. Anyway"—her voice lowered to a faint whisper— "whatever you do, don't tell my father anything about—"

"I do apologize. Updates regarding Berenza's efforts." The archduke had stridden back across the hall with tremendous pace. He sat again at the table's head and sipped from his wine goblet. The elaborate silver shimmered under candle flickers.

"Any wor—"

"Nothing on your friend yet, I'm afraid. But the net is already closing on those three villains. Oh, and Annabelle"—he plucked two grapes from their pale cluster and spoke through chews— "you are not to leave the castle unaccompanied under—"

"Not even to the lake?"

"The lake is where you would have been abducted"—he nodded at Jack— "if not for this young man's intervention. I should have thought you would be less than keen to return."

"I won't let scoundrels like them dictate my schedule, thank you very much!" she said in sharp reply, huffing and wrapping her arms in a tight fold of silken frills.

Jack was grinning—internally—at her tenacity. She had guts.

Wiping his hands on a thick linen napkin, Archduke Oakenfol let out a sigh before smiling at Jack. "As you can see, I spoil my daughter. I do apologize." His focus shifted to Annabelle. "Fine then. If you insist, Magnus will escort you to and from the lake. He will guard out of sight, to give you your privacy. I will instruct—"

"Magnus? Oh, please not him. He's a frightful bore." Her amber eyes fluttered at Jack, then, with fluffy ear tips crinkling, she looked up at the candelabra, bobbing her furry neck side to side as if musing. Waving a casual backhand, she said, "Perhaps Jack could—"

"No. Now, I think today's events have left you exhausted. An early night will do you the world of good."

"Father, please, it's so early. I want to know more about Jack and—"

"No. Off to bed with you. Now."

"I'm not a child. I'm a grown—"

"You are my child, and you will do as I say. And don't talk back to your father. You've been doing that all too often, lately. Go on now, off to bed with you. Immediately, young lady."

She gave a final defiant tut. "Fine." Her tone softened as she looked at Jack. "Well, goodnight then. Thank you again for rescuing me. We will see each other tomorrow, I hope?"

"Sure, sounds good. Goodnight, princess."

She left the hall with her leather slippers gliding across the flagstones in faint scrapes.

"Now, Jack, why don't we retire to the Grand Salon for a drop or two of rum? I suspect there's a lot more to you than meets the eye, and I'm keen to hear all about it."

He hoped he'd find a suitable opening in the

conversation to discuss Annabelle's makeover without causing offence. Ditto for the missing arm.

❋ ❋ ❋

"An assault on my family"—he sucked another slurp from his small tankard of rum— "right outside these walls. I didn't think anyone would dare." He stared into his drink, tipping the vessel side to side, as if simpler times hid between the sloshes.

The Grand Salon was an enormous semi-circle, decked in red leather, mahogany and marble. Two parts of its circular wall were lined in tall bookshelves, crammed full of volumes bound in brown and black. Jack peered, trying to make out the titles; the gold foil lettering on their bindings was small, worn, and impossible to read despite plentiful candlelight. The third wall section, the central one, was gleaming glass, through which Jack could see the chunky balustrade of an enormous torch-lit terrace.

They were sitting in the middle of the room, beside its roaring hearth. Logs spat in sporadic angry pops as flames licked and crackled, bathing the heaped wood inside its ash-dusted iron basket.

Jack rolled his sleeves high and braced trainer treads on the shiny white floor, pushing the chair's chunky wooden legs back for precious inches of respite. The archduke seemed impervious; his face staying pale despite proximity to the furnace. He could feel his own cheeks pulsing.

High above the hearth hung something he realized he'd never seen inside a painted world before: another painting. It was of an imposing man, armoured in plate and chainmail. He had an enormous broadsword clutched in both hands and bodies of fallen warriors littered the ground around him. His thick brown beard and swarthy skin gave him a pirate look—like Blackbeard—though the battle was portrayed without any water in sight. Whoever he was, Jack was sure his fame came from fighting.

"Any idea who would have wanted to hurt Annabelle?" Jack asked as he gyrated his cup. A pungent blend of notes resembling coffee, ginger and herbs rose from among the liquid's dark swirls. The archduke had poured him far too much. He took a sip—the tiniest token of one—and tried to mask his discomfort as spicy heat engulfed his tongue.

"Remnants, most likely. Or just exceptionally stupid criminals. Perhaps both. Either way, it wasn't her they wanted to hurt. She has no enemies. She's never harmed anyone—or anything

—in her entire life. Won't even so much as feast on roast chicken. Imagine, her, an Oakenfol, and unable to"—he looked up from his tankard and smiled—"but never mind that now. Tell me more about yourself."

Jack didn't know what remnants the archduke was talking about. A change of subject was welcome. "Of course, what would you like to know?"

He tipped the tankard yet again, and then rested it on the chair arm, circling his index finger along its silver rim. "Tell me where you're from."

"Oh, one of the villages on the edge of the forest."

"Which forest would that be?"

"The uh—"

"The Poets' Forest, I suspect. A lot of artistic types seem to come from over that way."

"Oh yes, of course. The Poet's Forest. That's it. Funny the things you forget, isn't it?"

He nodded, blue eyes shining above a broad smile. "Indeed. And the name of your village?"

"You wouldn't know it. It's tiny. Takes ten seconds to walk through."

"I see. Well, I don't know the names of any of the smallest villages around that area if I'm being honest. But I am always happy to expand my geographical knowledge. Especially as I am"—he outstretched his solitary arm, pointing towards the wall of glass with combined fingertips— "the ruler of these lands."

"Of course. It's called...London." Preposterous, but the name had popped into Jack's head and straight out his mouth.

"London"—he slowed the two syllables, savouring them— "London. Interesting name. And tell me, what do you think of that, being that you're a painter?" He gestured with eyes to the painting.

"I'm fascinated by its subject. Is he a relative of yours?"

The archduke's eyelids peeled, emphasizing strikingly bright irises. He stared with a paper-thin smile before swigging from his tankard. Placing his drink back on the chair's arm, he pointed his index at Jack, flicking it with gentle wags. "You are an interesting young man, aren't you, Jack? No, he wasn't a relative. He"—the archduke eased back in his chair, breathing out a sigh— "was Count Brackenbridge."

"Count Brackenbridge? Cool name. Was he your friend then?"

The archduke's eyebrows furrowed, his face screwing as if Jack had claimed grass was pink and the night sky tangerine. "You're actually serious. You've genuinely never heard his name before, have you?"

Jack nodded. The answer was obvious; he wouldn't insult the man's intelligence. "I haven't."

His facial muscles contorted, seeming to

wrestle between confusion and amusement. "Count Brackenbridge was the leader of the Great Rebellion." He was scanning Jack's reaction with narrowed eyelids. "The one which shook these lands to their very foundation. He was the man who did this." He nodded down at the silk swaddled stump below his right shoulder.

"I'm confused, archduke."

"That makes two of us. And call me Cedric, please. It's a novelty to be addressed by one's first name when you're in my position. Let us speak as equals, friends, yes?"

"Thank you, Cedric, I appreciate it. So, ok, first, to clarify, he rebelled against you. Why?"

"Why does anyone? Did you never rebel as a child, Jack? Against parents? Teachers?"

"I suppose, but that's hardly the same." He realised he'd been obedient his whole life. He'd only ever been a rebel internally.

"And why's that?"

"Rebellious children don't usually start wars and chop people into pieces with massive swords, for one thing."

He nodded in agreement. "No, they don't. But the principle for their rebellion is still the same as anyone's: discontent with authority. That was the case with Count Brackenbridge. He didn't feel I was a suitable ruler and thought he could do better. Simple as that."

The hearth's fierce heat was dissolving the logs, turning their gnarled bark charred and cracked, collapsing them into a bed of luminous red chunk and ash. His jeans and sweater were toast warm, the heat from their fibres massaging his muscles as he sipped the rum. The spirit prickled his lips and mouth, but there was a pleasant easing in his neck and shoulders as it took effect. He had larger sips, feeling increasingly comfortable in Cedric's company.

"So, this Brackenbridge guy, he tried to overthrow you, and chopped off your arm, but you have a big portrait of him on your wall?"

Cedric sipped and sighed as if he'd had the same conversation before. "I do."

"But he tried to kill you?"

He shook his head. "Not exactly. Once my sword arm was cleaved, I fell, writhing in the muck, bested and bleeding profusely, him standing over me. With his heavy blade raised high, I expected a swift death. Hoped for it, in fact. But he lowered his sword. He pronounced my reign over and that my wounds would be tended, and I would then be banished across the other side of the Titans, to God knows where. He wanted me to live with the shame"—he gazed at the portrait, smiling alongside small nods— "because Brackenbridge knew the real punishment for men like him and I—great men—is not death, but shame."

"So, ok, if he beat you, why's he not sitting here now, instead of you? Did the tide of the battle turn? Your army managed to rally?"

"No, my army was largely diminished, scattered and surrendering."

"Then how did you win?"

"The day was saved just in time."

"Saved by…?"

"A friend."

"Woah, nice friend."

"Yes, I thought so too."

"One of your generals?"

"You might say that, yes. A warrior with no equal."

"And he killed Count Brackenbridge?"

"He did. And when the rebels saw Brackenbridge's swift demise, their discipline crumbled, and they retreated, leaderless."

"Incredible. I'd like to meet this mighty warrior if he's in the castle?"

Cedric shook his head gently. "He doesn't live in the castle. But we'll see. You may yet meet him."

"I'd like that, thanks. But, anyway, I wouldn't keep a portrait of someone who did all those terrible things to me. Doesn't seem logical. No offence of course, Cedric."

"Mhm, illogical. Ok." He reached over to the tall stack of chopped log chunks and tossed one into the hearth's thick blanket of glowing embers. Hissing flames licked up its sides, engulfing it. "I've lived my life not beholden to what others deem logical or illogical. Easy to say as the archduke—of course—but I feel sure it would have been the same had I been a soldier, a baker or even a painter, such as yourself. And, oh"—he picked up the bottle of rum and pointed its top in a gesture of offer— "some more?"

Jack peered into his tankard, surprised to see it empty. The tension in his body had disappeared and his stomach glowed with comforting warmth. A little more wouldn't hurt. After all, he had almost been hacked to death earlier in the day. It was medicinal. "Just a little then, please, Cedric."

Cedric poured and the black liquid glugged, sploshing against the tankard's insides. Far too much, but whatever. He was feeling good. He liked listening to Cedric speak. It reminded him of conversations with Dante.

"So, Jack, let me ask you something, regarding this so-called flawed logic of mine: Is a lion your friend or your enemy?"

"What do you mean?"

"It's not a trick question. Just tell me, if you were walking in the forest and happened upon a lion, would you view it as a friend or an enemy?"

"An enemy."

"Mhm. And why would that be?"

"It would kill me."

He drew his head back a fraction, frowning. "Oh, no. Much more than that, surely? It would devour you, would it not?" He placed so much stress on the word devour that it conjured images of a lion carrying out the action.

"Well, I suppose it—"

"It would take everything from you. Blood, muscle and everything in between. Then dump you out afterwards in a foul-smelling heap, without a second thought. Would it not?"

"I suppose it would, yes."

"And yet, what are your emotions if you imagine a lion in your mind's eye? Do you feel disgust? Hatred?"

"No."

"What then?"

"Admiration. Respect."

"For what?"

"Its strength, majesty, prowess. I suppose, even the fact I know it could—and would—kill me."

"So, a lion is your mortal enemy, but you still admire and respect it?"

"I do."

Cedric smiled and nodded at Brackenbridge's portrait. "Understand better now?"

"Yes, I do." Jack had been led towards a new perspective and once again it brought back pleasant memories of Dante.

"Good lad. I must say though, I thought everyone would know the history of the Great Rebellion. Even people in London. In fact,"—he reached across the nearby table, picking up and pouring more rum from its opaque, unlabelled bottle— "I'm certain they would. As certain as I am there's no Poets' Forest or village called London."

"Oh."

"When Berenza interrupted dinner, his primary intention was to update me about the hunt for Annabelle's attackers. However, he also informed me of reports he'd heard"—he raised eyebrows at Jack— "of an unusually dressed young lad. Handsome, black of hair, he was rumoured to have cured a man's affliction by the roadside. As if by magic, using paintbrushes he carried in a leather knapsack. You wouldn't know anything about that, would you?"

Cedric overflowed with wisdom, maturity. He'd offered to help in the search for Dante. He even showed empathy for the man who'd both chopped off his arm and tried to steal his throne. Rum tipples having loosened his lips, Jack decided to confide. "The rumours are true. It was me."

Shifting in his chair, Cedric's cheeks had finally begun to pinken. "If we are to be friends, we must tell each other the truth. Agreed?"

"Agreed." But how much truth was digestible? He didn't want Cedric to choke on it.

"Who are you, Jack? You're clearly not just some lowly painter selling pretty pictures. You have a tantalising mystery to you. I would know the truth behind it. Do me that courtesy, please."

"A wise friend once told me to be wary of people's reaction to the truth. It's those words that are causing some hesit—"

"Your friend was indeed wise, but sometimes we have to trust in others. Trust in me, Jack. Tell me the truth. The whole truth. Who are you and where are you really from?" Cedric was leaning forward, his blue eyes wide, fastened on Jack's.

"Ok then if you insist. I am a painter, but not like one you've ever met before."

"Go on."

"You're going to think I'm drunk."

Cedric snorted and smiled. "I think you are a little drunk, aren't you? But no matter, I've always believed rum brings out the truth. So, go on, please. Tell me what's so special about your painting abilities."

"What's so special is that I can create worlds with them."

"Worlds? What kind of worlds?"

Jack held his palms outstretched and gestured around the salon. "Like the one we're sitting in."

Cedric laughed and had a mouthful of rum. "So, you're saying you created the world?"

"I told you you'd think I was drunk."

"You are drunk, and that's as may be, but I also think you sincerely believe you're telling the truth, correct?"

"I am telling the truth. I know that must be extremely hard to get your head around, but you did insist I tell you the whole truth."

"So, let me be clear on what you perceive to be the truth: you think you created the world and everything in it, using your paintbrushes?"

"This particular world, yes. Although I didn't create everything directly. I painted a masterpiece, wishing for certain things to be within it, the unseen things, such as my friend—actually, since we're dropping all pretence now—my father, Dante De Luca. As it turns out though, the painting has taken on a life of its own, in ways I would never have wished. Now I don't know whether Dante's even here or not."

"What you're saying is that right here and now, we're sitting in a painting? One of your paintings?"

"Yes, we definitely are."

"So then, directly or not, you, having created the painting, in a way, created me too?"

"Yes. Unintentionally, but yes. Now that I've got to know you though, I can say I'm glad I did."

Cedric raised his tankard in salute. "I'm glad too. So glad I was worth the effort, thank you very much."

"You definitely were. I'm just sorry my masterpiece was flawed. This world was supposed to be perfect."

"Indeed, if only it were perfect. I would still have two arms. You do understand, Jack, that what you're telling me sounds—speaking frankly—utterly fantastical, from my point of view, don't you?"

"I can understand it sounds utterly bonkers from your point of view, but it's true."

"And where does our world's painting hang? Above a fireplace too?"

"No, it's hanging in the most amazing art gallery ever. It's called the Gallery of Galleries."

"Mhm, and where is this spectacular gallery?"

"In my home, in a place called Scotland. It's hard to explain. It's in another dimension entirely."

"Well, I do hope the painting's safe. I should be most upset if we were stolen, or, far worse"— he nodded at the flames— "burnt to cinders." Cedric's facial expression and tone were dry as the ash coating the hearth.

"Don't worry, all the paintings are guarded under high security and safety measures. You don't believe me though, do you?"

"I believe you aren't lying to me. At least, not intentionally. But you, of course, understand that to simply accept what you're telling me as true would be to reject every truth I've ever known. However,"—Cedric nodded to himself, his eyes searching in circles above pouting lips— "you did, if the reports are to be believed, heal a man in such a way both he and his daughter were convinced you had magical powers. So, there's clearly something special about you."

Jack nodded at Cedric's missing limb. "I don't use magic. I'm not a wizard. I'm a painter. If I were to paint you a new arm from thin air, would that convince you I'm not delusional?"

"Paint a new arm from thin air? That would be a form of magic, would it not? I mean to say, how in blazes can you paint someone as if they were a canvas?"

He stretched his arms wide, pointing around and upwards. "This whole place is one giant canvas to me. I can paint anywhere inside it, including on myself or other people. Including you too."

"Very well then, a new arm it is."

* * *

The satchel's bamboo box was open, and all its contents arranged on a nearby table. Jack was going to do such a breath-taking job; his host wouldn't be able to do anything but accept the truth.

Cedric had removed his silk doublet and was sitting with a bare upper body. Pectorals and abdominals twitched in definition under milk skin. His shoulders were thick and powerful too. The arm that had survived Count Brackenbridge was brawny, with biceps and triceps interwoven in buff definition.

He spoke while looking at the stump. "Having lost it before, I shouldn't want to lose it again. Flesh is so vulnerable, don't you think? Any suggestions?" His tone was coated in sarcasm, but his eyes were betraying nervous hope.

"I can make you a special one, made in a way so it won't be vulnerable like a normal arm."

"Really? You can do that?"

Jack nodded at his tools. "I can do anything, so long as I have these. I'll make you an arm that feels just like your real one but is made of tough metal. What kind—"

"Steel."

"Ok, su—Oh, wait a minute, I know. How about titanium? It's as strong as steel but half the weight."

"Titanium, eh? Fine. I like the name. Sounds like it comes from within the Titans."

"The Titans?"

"The mountains on the edge of the Known Lands. Surely you remember making them?" The question was wry, but not malicious. He did remember painting them; he'd just not given them a name.

Cedric was about to lose the sarcasm. Jack pulled his chair closer and squeezed silver paint onto the pallet, ready to craft a new arm for a new friend. "Do you just want the metal? Any decorations? Some gemstones on the hand might look good?"

"Oh, yes, thank you very much. Yes, why not, assuming they're free of charge. Why not an assortment?"

"Fine. And try not to freak out as the arm starts to take shape. If you fidget it'll be harder to paint."

He held his tankard of rum up. "Sounds like I'll have to make use of this then."

Jack began. He started with a medium-sized brush, forming the thin outline of an arm—a muscular one—in the air, attached to Cedric's shoulder in correct proportion. Then he chose a larger brush and began to fill the gap with broader strokes. A titanium limb was rapidly forming.

"As I paint, my emotions and thoughts transfer down the brush into my work. Some consciously, others subconsciously. Right now, I'm wishing the titanium flawless and for the joints to move smoothly and silently, just like a normal arm. The key is positivity while the brush strokes the canvas. That makes for an optimum result. It's coming up very nicely now. Do you like it so far?"

Mouth agape, Cedric nodded in silence. Eyes bulging in their sockets, his chest rose and fell in deep rhythm. His brow was beaded in sweat. The dry quips had dried up. He gulped rum and said nothing.

Jack studded the hand's knuckles, back and wrist in a tasteful pattern of black star sapphire, diamond and alexandrite. The diamonds and sapphires glinted, while the alexandrite's shade flitted between purple and pale green as Jack held and turned Cedric's metal digits, doing minute details in meticulous flicks and dabs. The sparkles blended in elegant harmony.

And then, after around half an hour of focused work, it was done. Cedric was whole again, sporting a stunning titanium arm. He stood. His eyes traced the length of his new limb, blinking, straining, as if he didn't trust what they were relaying to his brain.

"My God, you've done it. You weren't lying." Circulating the joints, he flexed metal muscle, curled gem-studded fingers and formed a sparkling fist. "This is incredible. Exquisite. It feels like I could knock a lion out with one blow. And it all moves just like a real"—he jolted, shouting towards the salon's entrance— "I shall wield once more! Guard! Guard!"

A soldier barged through the door in shiny chainmail, hand clasped on sword handle. He came to a sudden halt as he was met by a shirtless archduke with a shiny new arm. "Your Grace, you—"

"Your sword, give it to me!"

"Your Grace, your arm—"

"Hurry up, you dithering idiot! Give me it!" Steel scraped as the guard yanked his sword from its scabbard and placed the handle into Cedric's open hand. "Good, now leave us."

Cedric began slicing, poking and parrying vigorously in the air, as if in combat with an invisible opponent. "I am alive once more!" After several minutes of swinging, he turned to Jack, panting and smiling broadly. "My instincts were right about you. But you say you're a painter, not a wizard?"

"Yep, correct."

"Are you sure? This seems like magic to me." Cedric stepped close to Jack, chest heaving and teeth beaming. He switched the sword to his regular hand, holding it downwards like a cane.

"No, I'm a painter. My power comes from—"

"You mean you can only work this wizardry when using those painting tools? Nothing else? Are you sure?" Cedric held his new arm up, admiring, flexing the fingers.

"One hundred percent sure. And like I say, I'm not a wiz—"

A sudden thud on Jack's jaw knocked him to his knees. The room was spinning, blurring. He held his face in shock as Cedric shouted for the guard once again.

"Take this madman to the jailhouse."

Everything around him melted into black.

CHAPTER 24

Jack was in a dungeon and despair.

He'd woken on grimy slabs smattered in withered straw stalks. Slivers of daylight were seeping through a solitary iron-grilled slit in the stone ceiling. There was a straw-filled mattress, grubby and falling apart, in one corner and a rusty bucket in the other. Those were the cell's facilities. The one he'd been thrown into, unjustly.

The left side of his jaw was tender. When he touched the skin it pulsed pain from chin to ear. On top of that, he had a hangover—the second one in his entire life—and there was nothing to soothe his sandpaper throat. A million pounds for a can of ice-cold cola would have been a done deal at that moment. The bucket's acrid ammonia reek wasn't helping.

He vowed he'd never drink alcohol again. Nor trust Cedric. Both actions were hazardous.

"Are you the one who thinks he's God then?" a voice asked from the pokey hall beyond the cell's black bars.

Jack stumbled forward, grasping the iron cage and peering through to see a short—he was a dwarf.

"What? I'm not God. I don't know where you got that from. Please, give me water."

"Pity, I was hoping you could make me taller," said the dwarf with a sneer. His red hair was clumped in greasy curls, matched with a beard in similar style. A set of long keys hung from his belt, jingling on a large metal circle.

Jack's head and jaw aches were joining together as one; he lashed out with a tongue drained of moisture and respect. "I could hardly make you shorter, could I?"

The dwarf laughed, a saccharin smile revealing gnarled yellow. His eyes shimmered with restrained rage. "Glad to see you've got balls. I wonder how big? Perhaps the archduke will task me with putting them in a jar at some point. Vinegar is the preservative I favour. So, keep making jokes. Just makes my job all the sweeter when it comes to suffering time."

Jack's neck was trembling. Fringe sticking to his forehead, he could feel panic massaging his scalp with clammy hands. This psycho was going to cut his nuts off. He had to get out.

Grasping its solid handle, he found the cell door—not surprisingly—locked. Maybe the bars would budge? His palms were slippery on their chunky cylinders as he tried desperate pulls and presses, but the iron was rooted firmly in solid stone, neither moving even a millimetre under the strain. "Let me out. I want out. I WANT OUT!"

Keys rattling at his waist, the jailer was struggling to speak through gasps of laughter. "That's not how it works, I'm afraid."

"Let me out. I haven't done anything wrong. I don't deserve this!"

"Stop shouting. Quit that racket, or I'll shove a red-hot poker right up your magic ar— Archduke Oakenfol. What an unexpected honour."

Cedric stood in the hallway, his blonde tufts brushing against the ceiling's mouldy stone. He spoke from the side of his mouth at the jailer, saying, "Leave us."

"Your Grace." He bowed and shuffled out the door, closing it with a loud creak and clunk.

"Apologies for Hugo. He does enjoy his job rather too much, I fear. Here, drink. You must be parched."

He pushed the tip of a leather waterskin between the bars. Jack grabbed it, pulled the small cork with a squeaky pop and then stopped. Sniffing the skin's mouth, he scowled at Cedric— Oakenfol as he'd call him from now on—with a trembling stare.

"If I wanted you dead, you'd be in a grave right now, not a prison cell."

Jack guzzled. Cool water tumbled down his gullet in wonderful cascades, reviving saliva glands. He replaced the cork, leaving half still sloshing inside the skin. A reserve, as he didn't know how long Oakenfol was planning to keep him prisoner. Or why.

His panic had reduced, dampened by glugs, but he knew being trapped within four cramped walls would ravage his nerves quickly. He didn't want to find out how dark the cell got after sundown. He had to try and persuade Oakenfol to let him go, somehow.

Wiping dribbles from his chin, he stared into Oakenfol's eyes. The stunning blue was now more ice than sky. "I paint you a new arm, so you punch me in the face and throw me in here? What the hell? Why?"

"You're dangerous, Jack. Mad as a flock of soaring swine. I can't let you go wandering around my lands. You carry a lot of potential for mayhem."

"Mad? I thought that"—Jack pointed to Oakenfol's freshly forged limb— "was to be taken as proof I'm telling the truth about who I am."

He was wearing a long-sleeved doublet of navy silk, fastened with three large gold clasps. He tugged at the right sleeve until it was halfway down his titanium forearm. Even in the dungeon's dingy space—lit by a few smouldering wall torches—the gems on his hand glimmered. "This is proof of magical powers, adept wizardry, yes. Hardly proof that you're God."

"God? I never said I was God."

"You claimed to have made this entire world, did you not? What does that make you if not God?"

"Bloody hell. I told you, I'm not a wizard. I'm not a god. I'm a—"

"A painter, yes, so you keep saying. Well, you are going to teach me this magical art of painting. Verbally, of course, through these bars. I won't be letting you touch your tools ever again."

"It's not that simple. What I have is a gift. I can't just—"

"Then you'd better come up with a way of simplifying it, hadn't you? Take some time, think of a solution. Otherwise"—his voice lowered to a whispering hiss— "I shall have no more use for you."

"How the hell do you expect me to teach you by—I saved your daughter, or have you forgotten that already?"

"No, no, I certainly haven't. Oh, that reminds me"—he turned and shouted down the short hall, towards the door— "Magnus!"

Magnus strode through the door, handing Oakenfol a sack. Its flaxen fibres were blotched in crimson, liquid leaking from the contents within. He dipped his bejewelled metal hand inside, appearing to clasp something.

"What's that?" Jack was asking but wasn't sure he wanted to know the answer.

"I granted you a favour for assisting Annabelle and you requested a search for your frie— excuse me, your father, a certain Dante De Luca, yes?" The words slithered from between smiling lips.

"Yes." Jack's stomach was clenched. He wanted to make use of the bucket.

"Well, thanks to Berenza's efforts"—he glanced down at the sack— "I can tell you; your search is over."

No. "What do you mean? Please. Please." He pulled at the neck of his sweater. The walls were getting closer, the air foggy, as his focus tethered to the blood-spattered sack.

He pulled out a human head.

Eyes and lips contorted in a mask of death, drops of red gunge dripped from its severed neck as Oakenfol held it close to the bars, grasping it by straggles of hair.

Jack gasped in horror.

Then relief.

It wasn't Dante. It was the sword-wielding attacker from the lake.

Oakenfol's eyes sparkled with sadism. "Berenza and his men searched every corner of the land, and this was all they found. Well, this wretch's two companions as well, of course." He dropped the head back inside the sack and handed it to Magnus, who was sporting a crocodile smile. "Your Dante De Luca must be six feet under. Assuming, of course, he wasn't simply a figment of your diseased imagination in the first place. In any case, he is not to be found."

"How can you be sure?"

"Because if he were, his head would be in that sack."

CHAPTER 25

The ceiling's rays had stopped their trickle. Shadows blanketed filthy surfaces.

Jack was slouched against the bars, close to what sparse lighting remained. Two wall torches flickering with meagre flames kept him from the panic of pitch black. Other cells lined the hall—three on either side of his—but nothing stirred in the darkness behind their caged entrances.

There was no sound except the torches' dull whisper and occasional hints of clank and clink drifting down the ceiling crack, from somewhere above. Oakenfol's minions doing their rounds on sentry duty, no doubt.

His jaw still ached—flesh wouldn't easily forget a titanium punch—but he'd drank more of the water and, exhausted, drifted into sleep, waking with renewed energy.

And the harsh realisation of his horrendous mistake. This wasn't Dante's World. It was—he didn't even know what it was called. He wasn't in Castello di Dante. He was in the rank dungeon of a despot's castle. Dante hadn't materialised. Oakenfol had.

Jack was trapped in a nightmare of his own making. He'd brushed catastrophe onto canvas and walked straight into it, with a smile. He wished Jaheem, whose doubts had obviously turned out to be correct, had blocked the way, refused him entry.

The question now though, was how to exit. Oakenfol had his brushes and paint. Probably locked away in a safe room, guarded by countless spear and swordsmen. It didn't matter. The tools were useless to anyone but Jack anyway. If he could get out of the cell and the castle, he would run—no, sprint—back to the portal and safety beyond it.

But how to escape the cell? The only way out was through the door, and it was locked. Keys for the whole dungeon hung in a bunch around Hugo's podgy waist. Curled in a cot at the far end of the hall, he'd been asleep for hours. Not that Jack missed his vile conversation, of course, but if he were awake, maybe he could be lured close to the bars somehow then Jack could punch him out and grab the keys? There didn't seem to be any other possibility. He would pretend to be sick then attack if the jailer got close enough.

Flexing his fists, he folded knuckles into tight blocks and aimed a few silent practice jabs and hooks into the cell's shadows. He imagined his swipes connecting with Oakenfol's smile. Jack had never hit anyone before, but the tautness in his wiry biceps, forearms and wrists signalled his strikes would be effective.

Dante would have been aghast at Jack beating up a person half his size—or any person, for that matter—but cruelty and malice had driven him to this point, given no choice. He hoped the dwarf would be careless and come within striking distance. "Help—"

There was a quiet knock on the hall's main door. Hugo kept sleeping. The knock was repeated, louder.

He roused, sitting and rubbing his eyes, then stumbling off the rickety wooden cot. Keys jingled as he opened the door with a clunk of lock and creak of heavy hinge. Jack heard him speak in that murmured way people did when half-asleep. "Who the bloody? What are you do"— his tone sharpened and rose— "Does your father know—"

There was a thump. Hugo collapsed on the floor, out cold. Stepping over him came a figure cloaked in black who took the circle of keys and strode towards Jack's cell door.

The hood was lifted back to reveal Annabelle's canine features, bright eyed with furry ears pointed upwards in sharp triangles. Her voice was hushed. "Jack, oh you poor boy. What have they done to you? Are you ok?"

"Annabelle, what are you doing? Your dad is going to—"

"Never mind him"—she inspected his face with amber eyes— "oh no, poor you. Oh, he is a brute. Let's get you out of here." Her slender fingers fumbled at the key bunch, choosing at random, poking their spindly stems into the lock and twisting. The door stayed closed. "Blast! The keys all look the same."

Hugo was stirring, holding his crown and muttering sleepy curses. He sat up, trying to scramble to his feet but failing. "Guards. Help. Guards. The prisoner." The words were getting louder with every repetition. "Guards. The prisoner. Help!"

Annabelle handed the keys to Jack and strode back across the hall. Pulling a small black club from her cloak, she smacked him across the head, knocking him unconscious again.

"Horrid little man. I caught him peeping on me at the lake once, from behind a bush. Can you imagine?"

"Erm—" Jack reached through the bars and tried a more methodical approach to unlocking the door, holding keys separate from the main bunch after they'd been used without success. On the fifth attempt, the lock turned. It's scraping click sounded even sweeter than Annabelle's singing voice.

She leaned into him with warm whispers and wispy whiskers, both of which tickled his earlobe. "Follow close behind me, tread softly and be extra quiet, ok?" Her perfume was a herby cocktail of sweet liquorice and ginger; about the only thing in the dungeon that didn't stink.

Jack nodded. Now he was able to look directly into the other cells, he saw no people. Only cobweb-covered skeletons in decaying rags. His gratitude was surging. "Thank you, Annabelle. Get me the hell out of here please, buddy."

With a dainty finger placed in hush symbol on her furry snout, she said, "Ok, but remember to keep your trap shut."

They stepped over Hugo's splayed, stubby legs onto the landing of a circular staircase which stretched upwards surrounded by narrow stone walls.

"Ok, wait," Jack whispered. Closing the hall's heavy door with a soft thud behind him, he rattled and sifted until the correct key clunked its lock shut. The alarm wouldn't be so easily raised, and his jailer could try the jailed experience for himself.

He followed Annabelle, treading as softly as possible. The staircase led them into an open, cobbled courtyard. The dull sheen of steel under torchlight alerted Jack to a sentinel looking out across ramparts, in opposite direction to where they crouched. A sword hanging from the guard's waist and a medieval-type rifle—probably a musket—cradled in his chainmail-clad arms encouraged Jack to creep with ninja-level silence.

Annabelle pointed twice to a shadowy area across the cobbles. Jack acknowledged. Fresh night breeze contrasted with the dungeon's stale air, but he resisted guzzling it with lungs. Even overzealous breathing risked alerting the heavily armed guard standing just a short distance from where they slinked.

They reached the darkened corner and she beckoned him down a winding narrow path. The moon was in full glow, the centrepiece of a glittering star blanket, but he still struggled to see where his feet were landing on the steep, uneven ground. He stumbled, knocking into Annabelle's shoulder. Saying nothing, she clasped his hand and guided through gentle turns and tugs. Her palm's smoothness was noticeable, even amid the current emergency. For all his swagger about ladies, he'd never held hands with one before. Considering she was part wolf—kind of—the soft warmth of her skin brought surprising comfort. She navigated the winds and corners effortlessly, as if darkness had no effect on her vision.

The path ended at a lawn about the size of a tennis court, ringed in stout stone ramparts. It was hard to make out their exact shapes, but he saw what looked like benches and barrels. Jack could feel clumps of unkempt turf and patched soil under his trainers. The place was a neglected alcove of the complex.

Annabelle stopped and stepped close. Her voice was less hushed but still low. "This is the feasting area for the army's junior officers. It sits empty all year, except for one or two festivals. I sometimes come here to watch the beautiful sunsets"—he felt the squeeze of her smooth hand strengthen a fraction— "by myself, of course, not having anyone else around here who appreciates them, or a husband to—anyway, come on."

She guided him up creaky wooden steps, onto the rampart walkway. Jack looked out over rolling landscape cloaked in black, mottled with hazy beams from above. He saw the opaque shimmer of a river below the steep walls. Far below. The rock face extended downwards in a steep cliff. How was he going to get to ground level?

"Help me with these." She crouched, unlodging planks in the walkway, removing and stacking them at the side. Jack copied, finding a broad section of the wood was loose.

"What is this?"

"My father doesn't approve of tavern wenches in the castle. I suspect some of the men see things differently. I literally stumbled upon this while watching a sunset one evening."

The section was cleared to reveal what looked like a bundle of nets underneath. Annabelle stooped and tugged, bringing up the rungs of a rope ladder. "I think this is used to sneak certain guests in and out, during feasts if you catch my meaning." She slung the ladder over the rampart and began lowering it as Jack pulled its coarse folds from the hidey hole, trying to avoid clatter as he heaved.

"You're a 24-carat commando, Annabelle."

"Commando? Is that good?"

"Yes, very."

"Well thank you very much then. You're not so bad yourself. You're quite—oh heavens, I almost forgot. My father has your knapsack locked up tight, I'm afraid. It was impossible to get it back for you. I'm so sorry"—she let out a snort—"he's a thief as well as a bully."

"I thought as much. It's ok, I just need to get back to the forest where I first came out."

"Came out? What are you talking about?"

"Look, I don't have time to explain, and I don't want you to think I'm crazy so—"

She tutted. "I would never think that. Of course not, don't be silly. You're a little unusual, perhaps, but then I've never met a wizard before. I—"

"I'm from another world."

She paused. "Oh, I see." After a few seconds silence, she hugged him with surprising strength. Her body was slender, but the bumps up top large, pressed firm against his chest. "You poor, poor boy. He must have hit you so hard. You've even forgotten where you're from. My father is unconscionably—"

"No, it's not like that. I feel fine. I—I mean yes, my jaw is sore—but I'm thinking clearly. Look, let's just forget it, ok? Is the ladder secured?"

She pulled on the rope and pointed to the open flooring. "Yes, with iron bolts, into the stone. Don't worry, I can see clearly. Looks very sturdy."

Jack could barely see a thing. He tested the anchoring. Solid. It was time to go. "Thank you, Annabelle. You're a sweetheart. I won't forget you."

"I know you won't. At least, not for now. Because I'm coming with you."

"Eh? Annabelle—"

"You saved me, and I fully intend to do the same. I don't want you wandering about in the dark alone, dazed and confused, getting hurt. I couldn't live with myself."

"I'm fine, really. And your dad will—"

"I don't give a hoot about him. He's horrible or hadn't you noticed? He wanted to steal your magic, didn't he?"

Jack nodded. "It's not magic, but yes. Look, Ann—"

"Hey! Who's over there?" A guard was standing at the entrance, holding a blazing torch and flintlock pistol. Its chunky hammer was cocked right back, and the oversized barrel pointed straight at them.

Raising her voice, Annabelle replied in an angry manner. "I am the Princess Annabelle Oakenfol, daughter of Cedric Oakenfol, Archduke of all the Known Lands. What business is it of yours where I walk?"

The man paced across the patchy grass, peering. "Princess? Is that you?" He climbed the wooden steps, which shrieked creaky complaints under his heavy armour and sword.

"Yes, of course it's me, you impudent man. And I don't believe I need your permission to walk in my father's castle, do you?"

He approached closer, holding the flaming torch forwards and squinting at their faces. Wafts of heat washed across Jack's forehead and cheeks. "Oh, of course not, princess. I do beg your pardon. I just didn't expect to see—" He was looking at the rope ladder.

Annabelle's tone softened, turning coy. "This is quite embarrassing, I'm afraid. This young man"—she ran a palm down Jack's arm—"is, shall we say, a secret admirer of mine." Her eyelids fluttered at Jack amidst the torch's flickering flames. "I prefer him to visit discreetly. You do understand, the sensitivity of the situation, I hope?"

The guard's jaw was slack, eyes probing, scrutinizing Jack. "I—"

"Because, if my father were to find out, well, I fear he would silence anyone who knew. His temper is positively murderous..."

Head nodding and Adam's apple bobbing, the man lowered his pistol. "Very well, princess. His Grace need not know of your night-time strolls with your gentleman friend. I will"—he held the torch closer to Jack's face— "you know, you look familiar, friend. Haven't I seen you—hold on, I saw you with the captain, going to meet His Grace. You're that wiz—"

Annabelle lunged and shoved him into the walkway's open pit.

Bang! The pistol discharged a peppery cloud into the air. Miniscule embers fluttered from the smoke like angry fireflies. Annabelle whacked the guard with the club and shouted, "Jack, go!"

He clambered down the ladder, grasping its bristly sides and descending the rungs as they knocked against the rocks in woody clunks. She climbed on soon after, her floating cloak billowing above him.

An alarm bell clanged. There were shouts, commotion. The whole castle would soon be alerted.

Jack scrambled on rope and wood, seeing the black shades below reach closer.

All he had to do was get through that portal. The problem being that dear Annabelle couldn't.

CHAPTER 26

It was nothing like the pool in his palace. It was flowing, for one thing. And three times as wide. Jack wasn't keen at all on the prospect of diving into its murky currents.

There was no choice though. It was brave the water or battle the waves.

Soldiers flowed across the fields behind them. They formed a sea of steel; plated, spiked and topped with swaying flames.

Alarm bells continued clanging in the castle. Looking back along the ramparts, he could see torch-lit lines of helmeted heads, their musket barrels aimed in unison. But no shots fired. Jack guessed they didn't want to risk the wrath of Oakenfol by accidentally shooting his daughter.

Trainers submerged in lapping shallows, he tried to persuade his well-meaning rescuer to save herself. "Annabelle, you should go back. They won't hurt you. Just blame everything on me. Say I used magic to control you. Say I threatened to put a curse on you or whatever you like. I won't hold it against you. You can't go where I'm —"

She was panting from their sprint; her floppy pink tongue contracting in rapid twitches. "I hate him. I hate that bloody castle. If I die"—she stood with hands on hips, scanning the river's surface— "at least I'll die a free woman. Please tell me you can swim?"

"Yes, I can, but—"

"Fast?"

"Yes, I—"

"Then you swim as fast as you can, ok? With all your strength, you understand? And once you're out of the water, climb quickly up onto those rocks there, you see?" The outline was dark —like everything else around him—but the rocks so big he couldn't miss them.

"There isn't a problem with the river, is there?" Distant steel was clanking ever closer. His question was pointless. He had to swim.

"Just swim fast and get up on those rocks, ok? You'll be fine. Let's go."

In they plunged. He swam front crawl, but regularly craned his neck above the surface to follow the rocks' black beacon. The foamy washes against his face were grit-tinged, faintly reeking of dung. Annabelle was two or three feet in front, carving a splashy path in strong, determined strokes. He heard commotion surging behind them, angry shouts, chink and scrape of metal and wood.

Jack scrambled onto the squelchy riverbank and stumbled to the rocks beyond, following Annabelle's shadowy form. Clothes clinging to him like a second skin, he stood bent over, resting tired arms on soggy knees, and sucking air into aching lungs.

He peered back over the river to see his pursuers had stopped several feet from the water's edge. Their weapons were readied, but they seemed hesitant, having no intention of crossing. Even the ones in light leather armour.

Collective flame flickers meant he could make out Magnus' stocky frame pushing his way to the front of the throng. Hands full with roaring torch and cocked flintlock, he squinted, but didn't seem able to pinpoint Jack's location.

Magnus was pacing back and forth, nervously glancing at the river's heaving flow, as if its muddy embankment were made of quicksand. He bellowed, "Wizard! There's no point in running, you can't hide anywhere. You will be found. Give yourself up now and return the princess. You'll be shown mercy, I promise."

Sodden, shivering from the wind's crisp caresses, Jack crouched behind a large shard of rock and shouted his reply. "I've already seen your idea of mercy. You and your weasel archduke.

You can stick your mercy right up your big, fat ar—"

"Arghhh!"

The water erupted, causing chaotic yells and thunderous gunshots. Jack peered over the rock to see the flailing, gnashing bulk of a monster.

A gargantuan crocodile.

It had crunched Magnus' lower leg clean off. His chainmail armour had been shredded like tinfoil. He was writhing in the mud, wailing, clutching his severed stump as it gushed torrents of blood—appearing almost black under the moonlight—while the other soldiers screamed in desperate terror, trying to fight off the beast.

Gun hammers slammed in rapid percussion, flaring billows of thick smoke and spark through the air. Swords and spears were being swung in frantic hacks and shoves, accompanied by shouts and curses. There must have been at least fifty men. Versus one colossus.

Bloodied, leaking, but not retreating, its gnarled head swung like a sledgehammer of tooth and bone, smacking and flooring soldiers left and right, mashing its jaws—the spikes inside big as swords—into their flesh, sending spine-chilling shrieks into the night sky. Head and tail thrashing, its hiss a dozen vipers clashing; it clamped Magnus in its gruesome mouth and dragged him backwards with a giant splosh, down into watery oblivion. And then it was gone.

Jack felt the brush of Annabelle's cloak pressed against him as she gaped with bright eyes glued to the mesmerising horror which had just played out on the river's inky ripples. Warm, salty breath tickled his cheek. "We have to go. Come on."

* * *

"You could have told me about that—whatever that thing was," he said from the side of his mouth, trying not to let dampness of clothing compound annoyance.

They were tramping down a broad cobbled road lined with stone walls. It was still extremely dark, but at least they were on a proper path. And Annabelle was leading the way with her wolf vision. He did hope, however, she would warn him if there were any more terrifying creatures to be expected.

"Leviathan. They're called leviathan."

"Leviathan? It looked like a massive crocodile. You could have warned me."

"I am sorry, Jack, sincerely, but if I'd warned you, you wouldn't have dared get in the river."

"I know, because I don't like giant bloody monsters!"

Her tone rose sharply as she flailed her arms out wide. "Who does? And I think a maybe monster is better than a definite dungeon, wouldn't you say? And anyway, they sleep deep under the water, on the riverbeds. They're attracted by vibrations and noise. We'd hardly made any between us. That lot did. Hence poor Magnus."

"Poor Magnus? Poor Magnus? I hope he made a tasty meal. The guy was trying to throw me back in that hellhole."

She tutted. "You shouldn't make light of anyone's death, Jack. Not even an enemy. That makes you no better than them. He died horribly. Oh, my it was so horrible. That's nothing to rejoice over."

"Well, if it's delayed their hunt for me, I'll find it hard not to rejoice. I didn't ask them to chase me. I didn't ask for any of this. And I can't believe there are massive crocodiles here. But then, what's one more monster in this screwed up world, eh?"

She paused in her steps, fell silent, and then kept walking at a slower pace with head looking downwards and jaws closed. They continued along the winding road in silence. Rose bushes and tree branches rustled in the breeze, but Jack and Annabelle didn't speak.

"Are you ok?" He suspected the answer—the real one—but asked anyway.

"Yes, fine." Her tone told him otherwise.

"Are you sure?"

"Yes, I'm fine."

Jack had grown up in the presence of tense tongues. They said one thing and meant the opposite. He wasn't walking any further with her feeling upset. Why was creating entire worlds easy—or, at least, used to be—but speaking from his heart so difficult?

"Look, Annabelle—"

"No, no, it's fine, really."

"No, it's not fine, because you're upset." He walked in front, putting a gentle palm on her shoulder, blocking her way. "When I talked about monsters, I didn't mean you. I think you're an awesome lady. I mean that. I think you're incredible. In fact, you're the only person I've met in this world so far, I can say for sure is *not* a monster. Ok?"

She let out a deep exhale and her voice softened. "Well, ok. If you really mean that, of course?"

He kept contact with her glowing irises. "I really do mean that. I think you're awesome. And thank you for rescuing me. I owe you everything. Just please, please if there's any more insane stuff on the horizon, warn me first, no matter what, ok?"

She sounded chirpier. "Deal. Let's hug and make up?"

"Sure, of course." Jack opened his arms

wide, and she snuggled into him, pushing herself tight.

Her scent was now a mix of herbal perfume and dungy river damp, which he hoped wasn't eau de leviathan turd. He heard her murmur something like "such a sweet boy" as her palms pressed on his back. Embrace lingering and tightening, it seemed like she wasn't going to let it end.

After a few minutes, he gently pried her hands away, flattered but tutting. "Were you planning on letting go at some point?"

She returned the tut. "What? Oh, don't be silly. I'm just not used to hugging. It's not my fault if—"

Starry black was crackling electric blue.

"Oh no."

"What's that?" asked Jack.

"Insane stuff."

CHAPTER 27

"It's a tempest!"

"What do we do?"

"Try not to die! We must find shelter."

Jack was clutching Annabelle in tight embrace, staggering against the batter and whistle of wind. Bushes and leaves were clapping in frantic flutters. Branches creaked and groaned, straining as the storm surged. The heavens hissed, turning dense with grey smoke, flashing sapphire dazzles.

Then the rain started.

Blue rain. Buzzing with electrical energy. Large dollops, bursting onto the ground like artillery, fizzing outwards in crackling puddles before fizzling into the soil.

"The forest! The trees will give protection," shouted Annabelle into Jack's ear, making it quiver and ring from her high pitch.

Hand in hand, they raced in sways towards the tree line, dodging deadly splashes. Scrambling over walls and leaping a stream, they tumbled under leafy canopy, hoping to find refuge among deep roots and broad trunks.

In the near distance, he could see blurred outlines of what looked like thatched cottage roofs amidst the trees' groaning turbulence. "Is it a village?"

"Yes, I think it might be. Come on!"

Wood rattled and wind howled as the sky sputtered and sparked. A hefty tear exploded mere feet in front of them, sizzling over carpeted tufts in slithers of voltage. One misstep meant instant death.

Stumbling along the grass path brought them to a hamlet of half a dozen houses in semi-circular formation. With their chunky window shutters closed, neither light nor life could be seen within. The rooftops had speckles of crackle and fizzle, but it seemed the forest's sturdy array was doing a decent job of blocking ungodly torrents. That didn't ease his desperation to get inside proper shelter.

Jack hammered on the nearest door. No answer. He tried the iron handle. Locked.

Annabelle was already at the neighbouring cottage, screaming and pounding on the wood. No stirrings there either.

Another two cottages yielded the same results, and then, finally, with both Jack and Annabelle shouting and banging on it, one of the doors squeaked open a narrow fraction.

A woman's voice croaked from behind the doorway's dim crack. "Who's there?"

"Please, let us in. Please. We've been caught in the tempest, ma'am," said Annabelle.

The door opened fully. It was an elderly woman, hunched and leaning on a weathered cane. "Come in then. Quickly now, before more drops fall."

She ushered them inside and rasped instructions to follow, hobbling through the dimly lit room and down narrow stone steps, clacking at their edges with the stick.

They found themselves in a basement, lit only by three chunky candles on a wooden table in the corner. Its gloomy décor wasn't much fancier than Oakenfol's dungeon. The beds on either side of the room were proper ones though, on raised wooden frames, swaddled in crochet blankets and even topped with real pillows.

Petals bunched in reassuring beauty. Daffodils, geranium and yellow roses were arranged in terracotta pots along the front of a disused central fireplace. Their citrusy bouquets freshened the air, layering rustic fragrance over ramshackle furniture and crumbling flagstone.

Propping her cane against the wall, the old lady shuffled to a rickety wooden plinth which held cups and a small clay jug. "Please, sit on the bed and rest. I'm afraid I don't have any wine. Would you like some water?" The sentences clucked from her wrinkled throat, but the words were clear.

"Yes, please. Thank you very much, ma'am," replied Annabelle. They sat on the bed beside each other. The soft material within its mattress relented under Jack's backside in comforting crumples.

She brought two full cups of clear liquid clutched in frail fingers. "There you go. You must be more careful next time. You never know when one of these awful tempests will happen." Her eyeballs were milky, like marbles. She spoke to the space around Annabelle, not at her. "There hasn't been one for quite some time, or is my memory playing tricks on me?"

"No, you're quite correct. I can't remember the last one, thank goodness. I hope this one passes quickly. We were almost fried alive."

His chest was still falling and rising in shaky breaths, mind alight with what might have happened. Tempest? Electrical rain? This place was bonkers.

Annabelle was more composed but fear still weaved between her words as she spoke in weary trembles. It had been a short but horrific fright and he was grateful for the thick stone and earth surrounding them. Even if images of crafty witches—feigning blindness and frailty—were niggling his mind.

Dressed in a faded and frayed charcoal dress and shawl, with bare feet caked in grime, Jack wasn't sure about accepting anything from her, but his throat was begging for refreshment. As their impromptu host was doddering back across the room, he placed the cup's rim under his nose, sniffing at the liquid. His trust reserves were running low.

Annabelle nudged him gently and tapped her snout with a wink and thumbs up, before taking a gulp. Of course, she could probably smell everything in the whole basement, clear as Scottish spring water. Her wolf senses reassuring him; he guzzled, finishing the water with a gasp as it seeped downwards through his body in cooling, calming massages.

After giving them more water and a wooden plate laden with thick slices of flour-coated bread, the old woman eased onto her bed with slow, shaky motions and lay on her side.

"Erm, I hope I'm not prying, but are you blind ma'am?" asked Annabelle through vigorous chews.

Jack devoured the bread. It was dry, but extreme hunger supplied a rich sauce.

"Yes, dear. I am. Since as long as I can remember."

"Completely? I do hope that's not rude."

"Not rude at all. My blindness is obvious." Her crinkled lips parted to form a gap-tooth smile. "As obvious as the fact that you're a sweet and well-mannered young lady. Just a simple fact. And yes, blind as a bat."

"Oh, thank you. That's kind of you to say. But, if you're blind, why light candles?"

"For my son. He's not here now, but when he comes back, I don't want him falling all over the place if he returns at night."

"Where is he?"

"He went off a couple of days ago. Off with his friends, working. He'll be back soon enough, I'm sure."

"Yes, I'm sure. Probably out earning money to buy you something nice."

She chuckled, easing her grey straggles further into the pillow. "Well, he is a good boy. Always looks after his old mother. And money is always welcome, being so hard to come by. What I don't like is him earning it up at that terrible Oakenfol Castle."

"The castle?"

"Yes, I heard him talking about it with his two best friends. They said they'd be getting a solid purse from the royal coffers. Making use of their military skills, I suspect."

"Your son is a soldier?"

"He was once. For a real leader. A good leader. Now he's just one of the scattered remnants, of course. Anyway, he mentioned the archduke. I don't know. I just hope it's not dangerous. That wicked man—"

"Yes, he is, very. I can—"

"That wicked man doesn't care about anything. Except his monstrous daughter, of course. Everyone knows that."

Annabelle fell silent and took a large sip of water. Then, voice soft, she asked, "His daughter? What have you"—she shuffled on the bed, clearing her throat— "heard about her?"

"The same as everyone. You haven't heard the terrible stories?"

"I'm afraid, I've—I've lived something of a sheltered life."

"Well, be sure not to go anywhere near the castle lake, especially after dark. I hear the wolf girl wanders there like a grotesque siren, trying to lure handsome young men with her voice—they say her songs are surprisingly beautiful—lure them so she can do vile things with them then devour them." The old lady—more like ignorant old hag, as Jack now saw her—stretched two wrinkly fingers downwards at either side of her withered lips. "Long fangs, like that. Like daggers, they say. She uses them to tear innocent men to shreds. Oh, a revolting creature."

Annabelle was staring across at the flowers, her eyelids pooling with liquid. "Perhaps, the stories aren't true?"

"Oh, they're true. My son saw her himself. Said he was lucky to get away. She tried drawing him in by flaunting herself, naked as nature—she has a human body you know—and singing her enchanting melodies. Thank goodness he's got such moral courage and strength. Or he'd have ended up between her jaws!"

"Yes, thank goodness—" Tears were dripping down her furry snout.

"She's evil. Many say even worse than her father. You know she's part wolf? A werewolf they say. Drinks the blood of babies too. The ugliest beast in the Known Lands. Oh, why would god make such an abomination? Anyway"—the gossipy old cow shifted on her bed, facing away from them— "don't have nightmares. Do sleep well, young lady. You and your—"

"Husband. I'm her husband." Where had that come from?

"Yes, husband, naturally. Well, try to sleep. The tempest will take a while to pass, I'm sure. Goodnight."

"Goodnight, ma'am," her voice flailed on the last syllable, stifled by a teary choke. Saying nothing, Annabelle turned and lay facing away from Jack. Shaking, she wrapped the blankets tight over her head; body heaving with muffled bawling.

Decrepit snores rasped inside. The tempest raged outside. From above the narrow stairwell, he could hear batter of branches and whistling wind, rattles, fizz, crackle and creaks.

But it was Annabelle's turmoil that wrenched at his nerves.

Jack had never been able to protect anyone in his entire life. Not his mother, not Dante, nobody. Now he'd done even worse. He'd created a world with infirmity, suffering and danger. An entire world he couldn't protect. The people in his so-called masterpiece had neither asked for nor deserved what he'd dished out. The nightmare wasn't his alone. He'd condemned others. He'd been a selfish fool.

And an arrogant one. Arrogant enough to think he was too good—too special—to have to accept life's cruellest reality: loved ones perish and are lost forever.

Annabelle cried endlessly. Curled in the foetal position, thick folds of knitted cloth concealed the wails.

He took off his sweater and hung it on the bedpost, enjoying cool air replacing damp cashmere. He adjusted the pillow, so it was firmer under his back. Giving her arm a delicate caress, he spoke firmly into her ear. "Turn over. Come here."

She turned, sniffling, her voice rising in surprise upon seeing his bare flesh. "You're—you're naked."

"I'm not naked, silly, I just needed a break from that sticky sweater. Now"—he tapped his pale, chiselled torso— "lay your head down here. I'd like to hold you."

"Oh, well, my face is all wet, I—"

"Lay your head down, please, princess"—he squeezed her arm gently— "I'd like to hold you."

"Really?" Her snout stopped its drippy

twitching.

"Yes, really. Come on, lie down."

She rested her head and wrapped a cloaked, slender arm around his waist. Her fur was soft, warming. Whispering in a distant, drained tone, she said, "I didn't ask to be born this way. No matter how I treat people, no matter how good I try to be, they'll always see the outside. The wolf girl. The monster of Oakenfol Castle. There's nothing I can do to change it. I wish I'd never been born."

He replied, "I'd like to pour that jug of water over her stupid head." And then smash that empty jug over his own, ever more stupid head.

She looked up, staring at him with moist amber gaze. "Don't you dare. I don't hate her. I don't hate her son either. I hate the lies and ignorance. That's the real evil"—she pressed her head against his chest again, cuddling tight—"and I won't let the evil win. I won't be the monster everyone says I am. Never."

Jack cradled her, smiling. "Even after all the terrible things she just said about you, you're still so ready to forgive. You're amazing. And, what she said about her son. I think—"

"I'd rather not think about that. Let's forget about it, can we?"

Yes, that was for the best. He suspected he'd already been introduced to the old woman's son. Or one of his friends. Either way, they were all—most likely—sans body and in a sack. Annabelle didn't need to know.

Her ears' feathery tip wisps were grazing his chin, tickling. Massaging them from top to root, they were like adorable velvet between his fingers. He stroked and her breathing slowed.

"I'm not your pet, you know," her tone was sleepy, satisfied.

"No, but I like playing with—"

"Well, I can play too. I can see all your muscles. Every single one." She ran a smooth palm over his chest and abdomen, lingering around his belly button, circling it with a delicate fingertip, reaching out to squeeze his bicep. The gentle friction of female flesh was a new and pleasant sensation, coursing tingles across his body. "How does a boy get so many muscles? Wizardry?"

"Nope, a world-class gym and powerful desire not to be a skinny kid anymore."

"You're not a skinny kid, that's for sure. Jack…"

"Yes?"

"You're the only person who's ever been truly kind to me. You realise that don't you?"

"What about Oak—your father?"

"His idea of kindness is twisted. He'd have me locked in the castle forever if I didn't complain endlessly. It took ages for him to let me go bathing by the lake alone. Now, after what happened there, I doubt he would again. But that doesn't really matter now, considering the circumstances. Jack?"

"Yes?"

"I want to come with you, wherever you're going."

That was a problem. "I do too. But only I can go where I'm going."

"Don't be silly. I can go wherever you go. Which forest is it you live in?"

"I don't live in a forest, but there's a gateway to my world in one. It's called a portal."

"Whatever you call it, I want to go there with you. There's nobody else like you, Jack. Nobody else in this entire world."

"I'm the biggest idiot in this entire world, believe me."

"Don't say that. You're incredibly clever and special but..."

"But?"

"My father has a man, his chief assassin and spymaster, Berenza. I worry you won't be able to hide from him. No matter where you go."

"This Berenza I keep hearing about, is he the one who killed Count Brackenbridge?"

"Of course not. That's not his kind of battle. He's not a vanguard warrior. You really don't know what happened to Count Brackenbridge?"

"Your father said his friend killed him."

"Murdered him. In a fight no man could ever have won. Brackenbridge was a very decent man. Most of the Known Lands rose to fight beside him, disgusted with my father's rule."

"A fight no man could have won? How so?"

"Well, how would you win a fight against a griffin?"

"Eh? Your father has a griffin?"

"Well, of course he does. Chikara. How do you think he keeps the Known Lands in line?"

"I thought it was with his army?"

"Armies can be rebelled against and beaten. Brackenbridge proved that. Chikara, on the other hand, well, I can't see anyone defeating him. I must admit he scares me to death."

"Chik—what?"

"Chikara"—she lifted her head, staring with granite gaze— "the Red Nightmare."

CHAPTER 28

Jack woke with Annabelle huddled in his arms. His bare chest was warmed by silky nudges from her head and neck, held against him. Tight.

The old woman was still curled in her cot, snoring like a chainsaw low on oil. That was all the noise to be heard. No clatters or groans of the tempest remained.

He looked at Annabelle, still asleep, content and cuddling. He was her place of safety. And why shouldn't he be? He'd created her. Inadvertently, and exactly how or why he wasn't sure, but he had. What was he to do? Going through the portal would mean him in safety and her in abandonment.

Outside of her father's—albeit overbearing and manic—protection, what would become of her? Not everyone had the same sight issues as the woman who had welcomed them in from the storm. Ingrained ignorance from gossip and rumour meant Annabelle would have an impossible time trying to make a happy life by herself. She had fire and gumption—buckets of both—but not enough to fight the entire world forever. Or even if she did, it would leave her miserable and twisted. Perhaps equal to her father. God forbid, perhaps even worse.

He wanted to take her with him, but Dante's words were firm in his memory: *Paint cannot leave canvas. Even an apple brought back through a portal will turn to ash in your hand.*

Annabelle as a pile of ash? He'd never let that happen. But then if he left, he couldn't bear to think of her as an outcast, mocked and reviled for eternity, imprisoned in the Gallery of Galleries. Her suffering this corrupt world and him enjoying the peace and security of Scottish palace life; their existences separated only by corridors and canvas. The thought stirred nausea. No, there had to be a way for her to find the happiness she deserved.

He placed a palm on her svelte shoulder and moved it gently back and forth. The cloak's black material had dried overnight and was like papery silk under his palm. "Annabelle, wake up. We can't lie here all morning."

She roused, tightening her embrace and replying in sleepy murmurs. "Just another ten minutes. These muscles are surprisingly comfortable."

He smiled and stroked her crown, enjoying the velvety texture. "Ok, ten minutes. Annabelle?"

"Yes?"

"Your father, he had a portrait of Count Brackenbridge in the Grand Salon. Do you know who painted it?"

Her voice was still hazy but becoming more alert. "I honestly don't remember. I just remember being sickened by my father's warped sentimentality. He had the man murdered, torn limb from limb and eaten by that evil Chikara, yet from time to time—as you saw yourself—he'll sit, staring in admiration, over a bottle of rum. It's disgusting."

"It is pretty messed up. The way he explained it, it made sense, at the time. He's very persuasive when he wants to be."

"He is when it suits him. And brutal too, as you well know. How's your jaw?"

"Still sore, but I'll get over it. About the painting: if there's a painting then there must be paint and brushes somewhere, right? At least, that would be the logical conclusion. Although I'm not sure logic plays a huge part in the way this world works."

"Any world ruled by my father will never make sense. I'm sorry, Jack. We can search the towns and villages, but the more people that see us, the faster we'll be running for our lives."

"If I could just get hold of some paint and

even one decent brush. I'd have a chance of at least righting some of the worst wrongs in this place."

She pressed her silken palm against his pectorals, massaging in circular motions that surged pleasure in his chest. "I can cope with the wrongs if you're here."

Jack jolted. "Of course! I've been so stupid. I'll go back through the portal, get another painting kit, and come straight back here again. And I won't be timid about using my powers this time. Even if it means violence. I'll fix things, I promise."

The thought of making it to safety and then leaving it again to face mortal danger wasn't appealing—was crazy in fact—but he would. For Annabelle. At the very least, he would be able to paint her a new identity, free of deformity.

"That won't involve you leaving me, will it?" Her head was tilted, eyes layering with a thin film.

"Don't worry, really. It'll only be for a few hours at most, I—"

The jug and cups trembled on their rickety wooden plinth. A millisecond of miniscule judder. Then nothing. And then again, the bed's wooden frame vibrating alongside the cups' tiny terracotta clacks.

Then again.

And again.

Jack had never experienced an earthquake,

so he couldn't be sure, but the pulsing shudders were rhythmic, as if from a living being. It reminded him of his first meeting with Samonoska, all those years ago. The memory was pleasant, but its current implications were far from so.

Annabelle bolted upright. "Oh no. Get dressed, quickly."

The old woman was stirring, mumbling through slumber. "What's that? The tempest still hasn't passed?"

"Ma'am, stay in this room and please keep quiet, no matter what," Annabelle's speech was rapid, the words blurting, muddled with urgency. "Come on, Jack. Let's go."

They raced up the steps with Jack leading. He turned the lock's thick iron key with a clunk, opening the door and stepping—into the point of a sword.

Its razor tip was poking the centre of his thin sweater with deadly precision. Jack grimaced from the sting of honed steel.

The weapon's wielder was cloaked in cream linen and smiling broadly under a pencil-thin black moustache. Parted pink lips revealed pearls in perfect uniformity.

"You! You get away from my Jack, you scoundrel!" Annabelle screamed at the man, lunging at him with her small club, only to be grabbed by two other men in similar linen garb. "Get off me! Let me go, Berenza you—you bloody bastard!"

The man rolled his eyes theatrically, tutting in loud clucks, mouth agape in mock surprise. "Princess, princess. Really, such language. And from a lady of the most noble birth. Shocking"— he smiled at Jack, turning the sword tip in a subtle twist, making him wince— "I may have to tell her father. You know, he despairs at her rebelliousness. You certainly haven't helped in that regard, have you?"

Jack was surrounded by at least half a dozen men. All in the same colour of cloak, two were knelt on either side of him with muskets aimed at his head. The others, bandeliers crammed with holstered flintlocks, had swords drawn, poised to strike.

The blade was digging into him. His sweater was moistening under the piercing metal, a small blotch of blood seeping through the cashmere. It would only take a moderate poke and Jack's story would be over.

But the sword was removed and sheathed. His captor bowed, smile dripping saccharin.

"Claudio Berenza, at your service."

CHAPTER 29

"Now, Jack, dear boy, the good news is, your troubles will soon be over."

Berenza's arm was wrapped around Jack's neck in faux friendship as they paced away from the hamlet, towards the forest's edge. Vice-like embrace and steely tone oozed effortless threat. "But I'm afraid—oh, please excuse me"—he signalled with an eye flick to the man beside him — "I'm afraid the bad news is there will be a degree—quite a high degree, I suspect—of suffering before you reach that point. His Grace seems to have had his fill of you. You shouldn't have run off with his daughter, silly boy."

A gunshot boomed behind them. The weapon's report was part muffled by stone walls. Annabelle, whose snout had been bound with a silk scarf, strained and whined upon hearing the sound, struggling and battering slender shoulders against the two bulky men escorting her in firm grip.

The old woman had hobbled to the doorway, questioning what was going on and asking after their wellbeing. It was her final curiosity. The other cottages' shutters and doors remained closed. If anyone was inside, they were wise to hide.

Parts of the forest had succumbed to the tempest; branches torn and splintered in jagged bristles, they lay strewn across the grass path Jack and Annabelle were being marched along. Trees were bent in swathes, as if smacked repeatedly by a giant spade.

Sap and leaf scents should have been invigorating, but the notorious assassin's clamp and grin saw citrus fragrances go unappreciated. Jack's neck was coated in sweat, the linen fibres of Berenza's sleeve scraping against him with menacing presses. He was paralyzed, trapped in a web laid thick by the heavily armed killers enclosing him.

Another vibration rattled the scatters of twigs and leaves under his—now scuffed and grubby—designer trainers. The walk's destination would be a fearful one. Something horrible was waiting.

❋ ❋ ❋

And it had wings.

Chikara. The Red Nightmare.

It was smaller than Samonoska, but that wasn't saying much. Its wingspan still rivalled an aeroplane, coated in broad crimson feathers long as hockey sticks. The leather tail was twined like a whip, trailing far back in mottles of maroon and burgundy. Black talons—curved like keen sabres—stretched in spikes from its feet. The ground shuddered with every stomp it planted into the meadow's flattened grass. Narrowing its football-sized ruby eyes on Jack, it released a screech somewhere between hiss and roar. Like a lion gnashing at a nest of vipers.

Muscles swelled under its red fur. Dark red, like blood bubbling from a pierced liver. Its massive beak and tongue were both scarlet, patterned with charcoal spatters. Stamping closer, it glared and screeched again, sending quake under and up Jack's trembling legs.

Helped by two other assassins, Berenza now held Jack's sweater in bunches, forcing him forward to within a few feet of the griffin's grim beak.

The dagger-like hook lifted high, hissing, heating Jack's face with waves of hot stench, the reek a sickening mix of rotting meat and dung. Even Berenza stepped back slightly, breathing through clenched teeth.

But the worst part was its mane. It was neither fur nor hair. It was woven poison.

Chikara's colossal head was wrapped in a crown of king cobras. Too many to count from where he stood. Jet black, they roamed and rose —large hoods flaring and closing—whispering in high-pitched malice.

A vile beast. And one of his own creation. Were there really horrors within him that could forge evil in such ferocity?

A second monster was mounted atop it. Smaller in size but no less venomous.

Oakenfol. Covered in plate armour—the shade matching his bare and bejewelled titanium arm—his flanks were blanketed with soldiers. Muskets aimed, swords drawn, and spears pointed; Three or four hundred men crowded across the landscape.

He peered down, smiling and stretching his arms wide in devilish welcome. "Jack, so good to see you again. You wanted to meet the warrior with no equal, as I recall? Well,"—he nodded downwards at Chikara's gruesome head-- "he's been keen to meet you too. Ever since you absconded. Haven't you, my friend? You don't like Jack very much, do you?" He stroked the mane of cobras, their dark sinews curling and writhing around his arms and torso in bitter hisses.

Jack staggered, dizzy from the thump of blood battering his innards. Berenza and the others tightened their clutches. "Oaken—Cedric, please. I—"

"Shut up, you conniving little devil!" His bellow thundered like cannon blasts. Then, eyebrows lowering, he hissed words as the snakes slithered between his hands and fingers. "He wants to eat you. Wants to see if you're as juicy as Brackenbridge, I suspect." Oakenfol looked round the hills at his soldiers. "What say you men? What parts should be feasted on first?"

"His heart!" Came a cry from among the ranks.

"Heart? Heart? This boy has no heart. He stole my only daughter. Bewitched her, wrapped her in his ungodly thrall. Turned her against me!"

Another suggestion was shouted. "His tongue!"

"Tongue, tongue. Hmm." A solitary snake rose parallel with Oakenfol's face. Its tiny black tongue flickered a fraction away from his icy blue irises. He ran a titanium finger along the side of its ghastly hood. "Not bad, not bad. But then his screams would lose their lustre, would they not? He should scream loudly until the last breath, begging and wailing for his miserable life."

Berenza released Jack into the grasp of his aides and stepped close to Chikara's side, looking up at Oakenfol. He showed no fear of the cobras' acidic hissing.

"Your Grace, I suspect it was—at least in part—the boy's handsome features which helped bewitch the princess. Her being an innocent maid, of course, no doubt made her susceptible to such charms. Perhaps justice dictates they be"—he moved his upturned palms in the air like weighing scales, falling and rising in opposite directions— "adjusted? And Magnus was a loyal captain. This little shit sat and watched him be torn to pieces by a leviathan. Might be there be some equal measure to be doled out?"

Oakenfol climbed down from Chikara in clinks and clanks, his heavy boots planting on squashed green tufts with a clunk. A huge broadsword was belted around his waist with thick leather, holstered in an ornate scabbard of gleaming steel.

Stroking wispy blond beard with gauntlet-clad digits, he smiled. "I like your thinking. Yes, I think"—he glared at Annabelle, the smile melting and reforming into clenched jaw muscles— "and you? You would betray your own father! What was it? A weak mind or weak at the knees? You'll never speak to another boy as long as you live. Your chambers will become your cage!"

Without warning, Oakenfol pivoted, punching Jack hard in the gut, buckling him. A terrifying fusion of breathlessness, thumping nausea and searing sizzles of agony gripped and dragged him onto the grass, wheezing and moaning. The pain in his jaw was petty in comparison.

Oakenfol commanded Berenza, pointing downwards at Jack. "You and your men are to beat that pretty face to a pulp. A bloody pulp. Unrecognisable. Do not kill him. Take him to the Madaka and tie him up by its banks. Wherever the leviathan lurk in greatest number. Let him suffer the same fate as Magnus. I want him alive when they tear him apart, fighting over his flesh."

Annabelle tried screams, but the tight scarf stifled, allowing only whines to sidle free as she strained against the men clutching her svelte frame.

Jack looked up from the mushy grass with blurred vision, stretching his fingers out, sputtering as he struggled to breathe. "Annabelle."

Slinging her over his shoulder, Oakenfol climbed onto Chikara. She was kicking, struggling with muffled wails. He sat her astride, beside the writhing mane, wrapping armoured arms tight around her flinching body. Snakes were crawling across her cloak in slimy slithers, causing her amber eyes to flare wild in their sockets.

"Alive." Chikara rose, swinging his wings in hefty beats, knocking gusts across the meadow, causing linen cloaks to flutter and flap. Oakenfol shouted one last time from above. "Berenza, alive!"

"With pleasure, Your Grace," replied Berenza with a bow.

Sucking air in painful shakes, Jack watched Annabelle disappear into the sky.

CHAPTER 30

"Oh, dear me, look at you. Drink this. You look as if you're about to die of thirst, poor lad," said Berenza, tutting and rubbing a gloved palm over Jack's crown, nudging the narrow tip of a leather water canteen into his mouth. He was crouched beside him, feigning concern. The most repugnant nurse in existence.

Slouched on his backside and able to breathe again, the pain from Oakenfol's strike was dulling from agony to sickening ache. He sucked hard at the lukewarm water. It brought relief, in relative terms.

He was still facing imminent death.

The sun—the one he'd created—was bathing him in mellow rays. Now Chikara was gone, birds were chirping again, perched in branches, content with the simplicities of blue sky and breadcrumbs. In the distance, he saw the majestic snow-topped Titans peaking high into hazy azure. Magnificent.

All his own work. And he was going to die in it. Inside his own failed masterpiece.

The polished wood of a flintlock handle was jutting from Berenza's bandelier, beside Jack's hand, within easy grab. If only he knew how to use one of the bloody things.

The regular troops had marched back to Oakenfol Castle. Now Jack was circled by the eight members of Berenza's assassin squad, or spies, or whatever the hell they were.

Berenza sat beside Jack. The sides of his white leather boots were smeared in grass stains and mud. And specks of red.

Placing the water into a satchel under his cloak, he took out another, smaller flask, pulled the cork with a pop, and tilted it to his mouth twice. Alcohol scent wafted from his lips. "Want some? Good stuff, you know. Spiced brandy."

"I don't drink."

"You know, Jack"—he placed a firm palm on Jack's shoulder, rubbing it— "I hate to break this to you, but you're not going to die of over drinking." Sniggers rippled throughout his men. "Go on, have a sip. It'll help. It always helps."

He shook his head. "I don't want it."

Berenza pursed his lips and nodded, sucking air through pearly teeth. "Refusing brandy before death, eh? You really are a mad one, aren't you? And you're a powerful wizard too, correct? You created His Grace's new arm from thin air, or so everyone says. But you don't seem to have any powers to defend yourself now. Why not? If I were a wizard"—he pointed with an open palm around the circle of men— "I'd have killed this bunch of slackers back in the hamlet."

Laughter erupted from the other assassins, causing squeak and clunk of leather and wood.

Jack didn't see the joke. "Is this how you always torment your victims before their end? Dragging it out so your men can laugh at your stupid jokes?"

Berenza took another glug and gasped in sharp satisfaction. "Oh no, not at all. I normally just kill them." He turned to Jack, supple cheeks raising in a dimpled smile. Eyes green, skin flawless and grooming spotless, he was a fine-looking man. A real piece of work. "Now"—he shrugged and rolled his eyes to the sky and back— "you probably don't think I'm a very nice person."

More laughs from his men. Berenza's chocolate brown locks were perfectly clipped and combed, with a few strands fluttering in the wind's whispering nudges; his emerald irises were sparkling under golden sunshine.

"Mate, I think you're a scumbag." He had nothing left to lose. It was over anyway.

Glugging from the flask, Berenza sputtered brandy across the grass, filling the air around them with spicy grape vapours. His coughs turned to heaving chuckles.

"Very good, Jack. That's the spirit. And yes, I do tend to get, shall we say, overly passionate about my work." He sighed, tutted and shrugged. "But it is a horrible way to go, isn't it? Face smashed to a pulp and then your body torn apart by a group of ravenous leviathan. It will be unimaginable suffering. I can spare you that fate. I'll do you a deal, ok? You make me something magical, like say"—he nodded at the canteen, sloshing the contents in light swirls— "a brandy flask that never empties, or eyes that can see in the dark, like the princess has, and I promise, promise—cross my heart—to kill you quick. You won't feel a thing. Of course,"—he shrugged again— "we will still have to sling you in the Madaka, so His Grace is none the wiser, but you're going to be dead by that point, so what the hell, right? It's a win-win."

Jack realised he was sitting in the presence of pure evil. "Even if I could, I wouldn't. I wouldn't give you a damn thing."

Berenza blew a hard breath through circled lips. "Ok then, I suppose we'll just beat you until your face swells like a watermelon—we're going to take our time doing that, I might add—and then feed you to the river monsters alive. You're going to suffer a lot, Jack. But I assure you, I will take no pleasure in—oh, who am I kidding?" He chuckled and nodded rapidly, taking Jack's cheek in gentle pinch. "I'll take a lot of pleasure in it."

"You're evil. You know that, right?"

He shook his head. "I'm just doing my job. It's not my fault if I love—oh, by the way, I thought you might like to know before you become leviathan dung. We heard reports of a strange light. Up in the Far Forest. A pit fizzing with bright light. We found it, quickly." He grinned with gleaming teeth. "As you know, we're good at that."

"You found the portal?"

"Oh, is that what you call it? Interesting. Well, anyway, with all those dazzling lights and fizzling noises, it looked a bit unsafe, so we assessed the danger, with the help of a couple of kids from a nearby orphanage. Brother and sister, I believe they were. Adorable little squirts."

The ache in Jack's stomach resurged, stronger. "Oh no. They—"

Berenza's cheeks contorted in mocking grimace, nodding, as if knowing Jack's question. "Yes, I'm afraid so. They went up like"—he bunched his gloved fingertips then flared them outwards— "puff."

"You sick—"

"Smelled like charred pork or similar? Wasn't bad, actually. Made me rather hungry."

Jack lunged for the pistol handle, shaking with outrage. Berenza grabbed his wrist and elbowed him in the jaw. On the part that was already tender. Torrents of sharp stabs flooded his face like a myriad of tiny daggers all jabbing at once.

"Well anyway"—he corked and stashed the brandy, standing and dusting grass off his cloak — "several dozen men swinging axes day and night means your magical barbecue is now buried under a few hundred tons of cedar. Not that it matters to you, of course. Gentlemen, let's begin."

He was grasped under his armpits and stood up. Berenza cradled his face with two delicate hands. "Don't worry, I'm not going to hit you." He grabbed his shoulders and spun him, pointing at a particularly bulky assassin. "He is though."

Wham! A blur of fist crunched him on the nose, sending him right back to the ground.

The man, who'd now taken off his cloak and was standing in a boxer stance, flexing chunky muscles and knuckles, was looking down at Jack and smirking. "Come on. Put up a fight. It's no fun if you don't try and fight."

The other assassins had unclipped their cloaks. Fists clenched, they circled him with hungry smiles, waiting their turn.

"Yes, come on, Jack. Let's see some bloody effort. Have some pride, man!" shouted Berenza from behind.

His nostrils cascaded crimson. The front of his sweater soaking, he put hands to his face to try and stop the flow. The liquid was gushing through his fingers, coating them and landing in spatters all over his torso.

Then he noticed something bizarre—bizarre even within the context of his apprentice life.

There was no metallic taste. As a boy at school, he'd been punched more than once by bullies. Bloody lip or nose, it didn't matter. What flowed always had the same formula: liquid tinged in iron.

The thug above paced closer, smiling like a coyote licking a piss-coated cactus. Sniggers mixed with snipes as they bickered over who got next turn kicking Jack's ass.

Jack rubbed the liquid between his thumb and top two fingers. It was gummy, gooey.

It was paint.

He stared at it. His fingers the brushes, he wished for a coating of hope. Not to die, but to save Annabelle and right the mistakes he'd made.

The crimson crackled, gleaming, bonding with his skin and wishes. It surged across his limbs, solidifying and shining. His aches and pains softened.

He stood, strong, examining his forearms and fists as he twisted them, marvelling at their glint in the sun's rays.

The brawny boxer was pacing backwards. Smirk was melting to slack jaw and wide eyes.

Bang! Jack felt a thud against his head, like a toddler had hit him with a golf ball. Turning around, he saw Berenza standing with fearful surprise and freshly fired pistol, a cloud of swirls wisping into the gentle wind. The killer's coolness was evaporating.

And then from all sides, he was barraged in bullets. Bouncing from his newly formed skin in plunks.

The smoke cleared. He was still standing. Swords sang as they were drawn from scabbards.

"He's turned to steel!"

Jack flexed metal fingers, closing them into a fist. A shining hammer.

"Not steel. Titanium."

CHAPTER 31

Strewn. Groaning. Begging.

The elite assassins had crumbled like biscuits under his fists.

Their swords and daggers had clanged off his metal skin, the swings growing more frantic with each failed swipe. Jack had pummelled all eight of them with ease; the strikes like lightning, landing in loud smacks, battering flesh and crunching bone.

Berenza's previously perfect teeth were now bloodied shards. Crawling on the grass in a feeble attempt to get away, he coughed out puffs of red goo. "Mercy, Jack. Mercy."

"Where was the mercy for those kids? Or that old woman?"

Berenza climbed to his knees, swaying and mumbling through sputters of blood. "Come on, boy. We both know you're not a killer. I see it"— he retched, drooling strings of red— "I see it in your eyes."

"Oh yea?" He raised his fist over Berenza's cowering face, feeling the power swelling, ready to deliver a final, devastating blow. To end a monstrosity of his own making. "Bet your life?"

His knuckles were taut, bunched into a pulsing block. Surging with deadly force. He drew his arm back far, aiming between green eyes which had delighted in the snuffing of innocent lives. Poised, he only had to swing.

Berenza was right though.

He couldn't do it. He wasn't like them. He wasn't a killer.

Instead, he marched his motley captives —stumbling and moaning—into a nearby barn made of mould-riddled walls and faded wood. Barely able to walk and terrified of his superhuman fighting skills, they made no attempt at escape. He tied them up with bandeliers and shredded cloaks. His new arms were incredibly effective at tearing and binding. He kept Berenza's cloak and sword for himself.

Once he was done with Oakenfol, he would let Annabelle decide their fate. In the meantime, they could suffer hunger and thirst instead of a bludgeoning into oblivion. That seemed like a win-win.

Jack knew his blood was paint. He didn't understand why but he knew it was true. What did it mean?

All this time he'd been searching for Dante as a physical person. But what if he were an entity instead? An essence? What if he had been right there with him all along?

The words from Dante's final letter repeated in his mind: *I will remain alive in your heart.*

He'd never know the truth of the matter, but he had a growing sense of not being alone. Dante had refused to be painted, to be imitated, and it had turned out that way. Perhaps his wish to live in Jack's heart had come true as well. The wishes of a painter carried extraordinary power.

And his ashes must have too. A painting made from the remains of the greatest painter was a first in history. Original. Maybe that would be reflected in what Jack could do?

He touched the temples of his titanium cranium and decided they were buttons for a hood. And so they were. He pressed them and the metal slid back, retracting effortlessly into his collarbone.

He decided the same for his hands. The metal was retractable gloves. Buttons drew them back to his wrists, revealing his regular pale flesh. Incredible.

Jack holstered the sword scabbard to his back and fastened the assassin's cloak. Taking the blade, he drew it across his palm to make a small cut. There was paint and sharp pain. He smeared the pommel, guard and edges in his blood. The weapon crackled for a second then shimmered. His hand healed within minutes, though a scar remained.

The sword was bulky, but he swung it with ease and skill. As if he'd been swinging it like a master all his life. He'd wished it so. For the first time since entering the painting, he didn't feel helpless.

So now what was he going to do? Berenza was scum, but what he'd said about the portal rang true. If it was blocked, there was no point in wasting time going back there, for now. He looked at his new armour and weapon. He wasn't afraid of Oakenfol and his soldiers anymore.

Chikara was a different matter though. He wasn't sure if any material—even titanium—could withstand the crunch of a griffin's beak. Or if his sword would do anything more than scratch such an enormous demon. He wasn't keen on finding out.

How to defeat a griffin?

He could try painting a rocket launcher from his blood. Except he didn't know exactly what a rocket launcher looked like, or how to use one. A machine gun. He knew the look, but not the usage. There was no way that would be enough.

Jack walked and pondered. His trainers had transformed into titanium boots. They felt equally light, but their treads flattened the soft grass in tight presses as he strode.

He found himself standing at the top of a meadow. Speckled in sunflowers and daisies, it rolled for miles in glorious green carpet.

When Jack was still a little boy, Dante had once told him of an artist named Jackson Pollock. He said he was one of the most famous -- albeit regular—painters of modern times. One of the methods he used was called action painting. The paint was dribbled, splashed, smeared onto canvas rather than being carefully applied. It had seemed crazy, just flinging paint around a floor. Jack had laughed at the time and said that wasn't real painting.

Dante had schooled him: *If the painting comes alive, what does it matter how it is constructed?*

Now he agreed. He had an idea. His heart was thumping with hope. It was time to believe in himself. Time for him to stop being afraid. And for his enemies to start.

But there would be a price to pay. He retracted the titanium coating along his forearms—after deciding on more buttons—and unsheathed the sword once again. Four stinging slices into the flesh of each arm saw paint pouring.

He lashed it across the grass in powerful flicks, forming the shape he had in his mind's eye. The ground was spattered at first, then red began to coat green, then cake it. Jack sprayed, dripped and splashed. He got on his knees, pressing and smearing with palms, fingers and forearms. More summoning than painting, he wished with all his heart for the only friend he knew who could defeat Chikara.

Jack was pushing well beyond the boundaries of his training, into the unknown. It was death or deliverance. There was no happy medium with stakes these high.

Crackles, hisses, crunches; the meadow was moving, rising. Coming alive.

Drained, dizzy from loss of blood, he dropped to one knee. His forearms had healed, wrapped in ribbons of scars.

The ground quaked.

And again.

Jack looked up to meet sapphire-blue eyes. Giant ones.

It had worked. Before him stood Samonoska. The King of the Griffins.

CHAPTER 32

"I'm sorry to do this to you, old friend. To take you from your home; to bring you here, a stranger in a strange land. And I don't know if I can send you back. I'll try my best, once this is all over, but I don't know. I'm not even sure how I did it in the first place, but I knew you were the only one who could help." Jack was standing with hands on hips, pacing back and forth across the meadow, dwarfed by the gargantuan sinews of Samonoska. "If it makes you feel any better, I'm in a similar position."

The griffin was listening alongside distraction. Striding in stomps—causing Jack's metal boots to vibrate—Samonoska peered around the landscape, his shining blue eyes roaming, searching. As if expecting a familiar face.

Jack shook his head. "I'm sorry. He's gone. I

think he's with us, I think—It's hard to explain. But I don't think we'll ever see him again, not with our eyes anyway. I'm so sorry. I know he was your father. He was mine too."

Samonoska raised his massive head upwards and released a terrible, drawn-out screech. Birds fluttered from branches and Jack—Titanium hood still retracted—covered his ears with tight palms. Then, lowering his beak, he nudged it against Jack in coos and hums.

Jack patted it, stroking the mane too. "I'm sorry. I got myself into this mess because I wanted him back. I didn't listen to him. I've been a fool. I hope you can forgive me for dragging you into this too."

Still leaning his sunflower yellow beak against Jack in soft nudges, he released a soft cluck and clack. The eyes signalling forgiveness was already given.

"Thank you. I promise I'll do everything I can to right all these wrongs. But there's another thing, I'm afraid. Another griffin."

The sapphire eyes narrowed. His head tilted, focused on Jack's words.

"He's not like you. He's covered in cobras for one thing. He's evil."

A roaring, clucking sound whirred from his tongue as the stare hardened.

"I don't know how I managed to screw up so badly, but this world won't be safe until he's gone. And his master too, a man named Oakenfol. I'm not even sure who's more monstrous."

Samonoska lowered his leg in ladder fashion. Jack climbed. He now sat upon the deadliest weapon in the Known Lands.

"Take me on your mighty wings, friend. In that direction, to Oakenfol Castle."

His purpose was clear. Determination simmered under his bulletproof skin.

It was time to save the world.

CHAPTER 33

It was all so much better from high in the sky.

Rivers, which brimmed with danger, flowed placid. Forests and meadows, a couple of which he'd almost died in, rolled lush and serene. Houses were clumped and cubed in quaintness, their white stone structures capped in charming thatch and terracotta. But not all their residents were as pleasant.

Whistling breeze, fluttering mane—its scent leathery, sprinkled in sea salt—and firm clamp of velvet-coated muscle around his legs; they brought back memories of his childhood. Flying on Samonoska with Dante, every moment fuelled by hope, wonder and mutual love. Happy times.

He looked at his titanium-armoured arms as he clutched the griffin's furry crown. Feeling the sword strapped to his back shift in scrapes and rattles, he reminded himself this was different. This was no joy ride.

The vast castle complex was drawing closer. He tapped all necessary buttons, coating head and hands in ultra-strong metal. Even his eyelids, which moved back and forth with the elasticity of real skin. Jack was going to need every millimetre of protection from all the potential death they were going to hurl.

Soaring near the walls, he could hear the frantic clang of multiple alarm bells. Samonoska's form—a flying fortress of feather and fur —would have been noticed from far away by even the doziest of sentinels.

Streams of rifle smoke flared along ramparts and turrets. Muskets in hundreds. For every dozen whistles past his helmeted head, one or two plunked. Samonoska got some of the bullets in his beak, spitting them out like miniscule knots of unwanted chewing gum.

Jack was trying to figure out the best place to land inside the castle, amid the zing and pop, when a massive object whooshed past Samonoska's wing, causing him to bank sharply.

Bombards. Belching out iron projectiles twice the size of basketballs. Booming, flaming; their gaping black mouths spat smoke and metal in tilted volleys as teams heaved and rolled bulky ammunition in rapid reload. Samonoska was twisting and dipping through the barrage, but one smacked into his torso, sending him barrelling, aimed like a screeching spear, fuelled by a titan's fury.

They'd really pissed him off.

Clutching the mane, Jack was ducking, hiding from more massive cannonballs flying overhead. As they hurtled towards the battery, the broad rampart blurred into smoke, thuds, crunches and screams.

Jack was strapped in but swaying in upward waves like a rodeo cowboy. He saw the carnage through clearing clouds of charcoal haze.

Samonoska had landed in a hurricane of talon, tail and beak. The stone he stomped on was cracked and crumbling, littered in corpses. Broken bones jutted from bloody limbs. Severed heads lay in misshapen splats, like coconuts freshly fallen from lofty palm trees.

Plate, mail, leather; all the armour was useless, torn like wet tissue paper. Screaming and retreating, the bombardiers who still had legs were dropping weapons and fleeing.

A fresh flurry of at least fifty musketeers poured into the courtyard below, lining in rows behind each other. They didn't get a chance to aim. Grasping chunky bombards in his beak, Samonoska began flinging them into the courtyard, causing shrieks and crunches as the iron cannons rolled and collided, squashing and smashing bone and flesh, sending the riflemen into panic, scurrying, limping and crawling in wails and sputters with muskets splintered and limbs shattered.

Jack surveyed the scene around him, gasping. Samonoska's rampage had drenched the ground red.

Then there was a thundering from above. The voice far more violent than any bombard's blast. It was the screech of another griffin. Oakenfol was flying above the castle on Chikara.

Beak and talons dripping, Samonoska bellowed in reply.

He soared towards their enemies. The battle had moved to the sky.

CHAPTER 34

The griffins circled. Far above ground littered in bodies and blood.

Samonoska had the size. Chikara the venom.

The Red Nightmare's tongue and mane combined in hiss. Samonoska focused on his prey. Silent, studying.

Oakenfol wore the same armour as before, but with an added Spartan-style helm of shining steel. It bulged in chunky triangular plates at either cheek, with a broad nose guard running between them. The forehead formed a sharp peak; a crimson plume flaring from its crest, trailing in a tail like fluttering feathers.

Jack could still—just barely—make out the glare of his frosty eyes. They seemed to be peeling wide at the sight of Samonoska, but a vibe of defiance pulsed clear.

"What have you done with Annabelle? Where is she?" Jack shouted over flap, hiss and whistling wind.

"You created a griffin, bravo." Oakenfol was twisting his head to keep eye contact as the griffins flew in circles.

"The King of all the Griffins." Jack's reply was bolstered by a screech from Samonoska, which only seemed to strengthen Oakenfol's contempt.

A smile peeked behind his helm as he laughed and looked down at the mane of king cobras, their hoods flared in unified rage. "You have to kill the king to be the king. Did nobody ever tell you that, boy?"

"If that's the way it's got to be, then so be it. Where is Annabelle? Where is she?"

Oakenfol's smile reformed into bellowing scowl. "Are you man enough to face me, Jack? See what you can do with that sword? Or will you try to depend on your so-called king?"

"Are you sure you want to face me?"

"Of course,"—he wrapped a palm over the bulbous pommel of his broadsword— "otherwise, how else shall I kill you?"

Jack pointed downwards in two solid jabs. "Down there." He tugged mane and Samonoska swooped, landing in a large courtyard.

He slid from the griffin's back, his boots planting with a firm clank on the cobbles.

Chikara landed at the far end. Oakenfol stepped off and stood, clutching his sword handle.

Both griffins soared, their wings knocking his metal skin in powerful gusts. He was confident Samonoska would triumph, but then nothing was sure inside this damn painting. Defeating Oakenfol would mean nothing if The Red Nightmare lived to chase him around the ramparts, unchallenged.

Jack unclipped his cloak and threw it to the side.

"I see you took souvenirs." Oakenfol strode to the middle of the courtyard. "Berenza and his whole squad defeated by a green boy"— he pointed at Jack— "and that armour, and the griffin." He was moving his helm in slow and steady nods. "It's true. I admit it now."

"Admit what?" Jack's hand was reached back, clasped on his sword, still in its scabbard.

Somewhere above them, talon, beak and fang were embroiled in titanic brawl. Screech and hiss pierced the sky.

"You created this world. It's clear to me now. You created it, Jack." He drew his sword in silvery slither, holding it in front, its guard parallel with the edges of his helm. His gravelly voice dropped even lower, the tone heralding deadly intentions. "But you don't control it."

Jack let go of his sword handle and threw both arms up. "Control it? I'm just trying to survive it! Now, for the last time, Oakenfol, where is Annabelle?"

His tone rose sharply. "In safety. Where I've always tried to keep her. Unlike you." He paused, in obvious wait for reaction.

Bombards thundered and muskets popped from other parts of the complex. He could smell peppery sulphur drifting through the wind. They were still trying in vain to kill Samonoska with conventional weapons.

"What are you talking about?"

"If you created this world, you created all its horrors too." He walked forward in cautious paces. "She's my daughter, and you made her deformed. That was your doing"—he pointed the blade tip at Jack's face— "not mine." Oakenfol rotated the huge broadsword effortlessly with his titanium wrist. "And yet she loves you and hates me. In what kind of world can that be called justice?"

"If you hadn't thrown me in jail and stolen my tools, I would have helped her. Just like I helped you!"

"Playthings! Are we your playthings, to harm and help when you feel like it? For your entertainment?"

"I've heard enough. Once you"—he pointed upwards with a shining index— "and he are gone, I'll—"

"How many men get to kill their creator? Perhaps I'll be the first." He moved towards Jack slowly, like a stalking leopard.

Jack drew his blade, clasping it high and close in both hands, uncertain of the imminent challenge. Also unsure of how to defeat Oakenfol without killing him. Maybe he would be left with no choice.

Their swords clashed in furious chime.

Scraping, clanging, battering; Oakenfol was wielding ferocious blows with his titanium arm. Jack was parrying with vigour, dodging and countering.

Jack took a heavy knock to his shoulder. The force dented his armour and staggered him sideways. He steadied himself against a stone column, gasping through metal lips.

"What's wrong, Jack? You thought I'd go down easily, eh?"

"Don't make me kill you!"

Oakenfol laughed. "Jack the Merciful, is it?" He lunged, unleashing a flurry of swipes and stabs.

Their swords clanged and scraped, clattered and sparked. Oakenfol's determined rage gifted boundless energy. Jack's titanium was tattooed in dents and gashes.

Dodging a particularly vicious swing, Jack countered and smacked Oakenfol's helm clean off, sending its plumed metal bouncing across the cobbles in clanks and rattles.

They battled below. The griffins above.

The courtyard shuddered, causing Oakenfol

to stumble a few feet backwards, stabilizing on one knee. Jack looked across to see Samonoska and Chikara atop a nearby tower, wrapped in a writhing web of talon and venom. The king slicing, the nightmare biting.

Huge sections of the tower's stone were crumbling under the griffins' combined weight, crashing to the ground, crushing soldiers below. Then, still intwined, the titans fell, smashing roofs and ramparts under thrashing tumbles of colossal rage and muscle.

Oakenfol advanced again, unsteady on the shaking ground, hacking and hammering, cursing, his pale cheeks pink, brow dripping sweat. He was finally starting to tire.

Jack dropped his sword and assumed a boxer's stance, bobbing and weaving away from the swipes. Without that helm, he could land a knockout blow. He'd let Annabelle pass judgement on her cruel father.

And then the dusky sky began sizzling blue. Bright blue. A tempest.

Oakenfol laughed through deep gasps. "Perfect weather for a day like this."

A raindrop exploded on the ground nearby. Jack darted backwards and Oakenfol made for an arch at the courtyard's other end.

The clouds were clumping, solidifying deep grey, riddled in electric crackles. Another two drops hammered in random spots on the courtyard, blackening the cobbles in hissing fizzles.

He ran in rapid clanks after Oakenfol, hoping to avoid any direct hits. He feared for Samonoska too.

Racing up a twisting flight of steps, he found himself back in the Grand Salon.

Oakenfol was there, standing beside the hearth, clutching a bottle of rum. He clamped the cork in his teeth, spat it and glugged deeply. Releasing a satisfied gasp, the spirit rejuvenating him, he shouted, "Here, boy, have a drink on me!"

The bottle smashed across Jack's chest, exploding in shards and stinking rum. The dripping vapours made him want to retch, but he had a job to do.

Beyond the salon's broad glass wall, churning clouds were lowering, transforming into dense fog.

Oakenfol readied his blade again. "I will triumph, just as I did with Brackenbridge."

Jack clenched his fists, ready to hook and jab the arrogance from Oakenfol's lips. "If you think I'm a god, why keep fighting me? I don't want to kill you."

"What kind of god doesn't want to kill? Isn't that the fun part?"

"You're twisted."

"That's rich, coming from you. Now"—he rotated the giant broadsword, pointing its tip at Jack— "come here so I can do what you're incapable of."

"I'm going to kick your—"

The wall of glass erupted in razor-sharp shatters. The battling griffins had landed on the terrace in their waltz of destruction. All Jack saw through spraying glass and crackling gloom was a flash of red fur and yellow beak. The fragile windowed structure stood no chance against their flailing tails and limbs. They struggled briefly, then tumbled over the ledge. Their fight continued.

As did his. Oakenfol was shielding his face with an armoured arm, the sword still clutched tight. Jack saw his chance. He launched over two leather sofas with a flying fist, aiming straight for—Oakenfol parried at the last second. The broadsword's flat edge clanged with brutal force, knocking Jack through the jagged remains of the glass wall, and into the smoky coating of the terrace beyond, onto his knees.

Recovering, Jack stood, desperate for shelter from the tempest, to get back under the salon's roof. But Oakenfol was standing at its edge, blade raised. A raindrop smacked the terrace's crumbling balustrade, spraying voltage in a wide radius. A splash landed on Jack's boot. It's electrical force rippling across his titanium in a million numbing punches, he was knocked into the heinous embrace of Oakenfol, who clutched him in a clanking bear hug.

With a crooked smile, he flung Jack back into the salon. Jack battered against the hearth's edges, stumbling. His neck lay in the large iron basket. No fire was lit, but the odour of charred wood cloyed his dizzy senses.

Oakenfol dropped his sword and pounced. Raining blows with his titanium fist, the gemstones were smashing in sparks and chips. Jack's hood was being pounded flat, tightening against his eyes and nose. The tempest's touch still had him woozy, struggling to recover, as Oakenfol hammered with manic energy. "I'll smash this helm into your brain!"

A sound pulsed from below. One that could tear clouds in two.

Oakenfol stopped his assault to cover ears. Jack's armour was vibrating. He knew it had to be the death of a griffin.

Then there were flaps and a thump on the terrace. The salon shook. The surviving griffin had come to aid.

With one hand on Jack's throat, Oakenfol —still with fist poised to strike—turned to see which champion would emerge from the fog's impenetrable swirls.

The tip of a beak was nudging through the grey. Speckled in black. Scarlet.

Jack despaired.

Oakenfol's eyes turned to Jack as soon as he saw the colour. Panting, he said with a twisted grin, "Looks like your friend wasn't the king after all, eh?"

But there was no hiss from beyond the fog. As the scarlet beak protruded further through the wrecked wall, Jack realised it wasn't complete. It was just the front section, hanging in frays, like a massive, cracked eggshell.

One being clutched in a larger beak of sunflower yellow. That of Samonoska. Eyes burning in blue fury, his fur and feathers blackened, billowing smoke from the tempest's blows, he placed his trophy silently on the salon's glass carpeted floor. His mighty limbs were shaking—shocks and venom had taken their toll—but the stare remained fierce, focused.

His head hung over Oakenfol with pitiless gaze. The archduke seemed oblivious, assuming the presence behind him was his red friend.

"You're not a killer, Jack. You can create, but you can't destroy. That doesn't make for much of a god, does it?" He pulled his arm back high, fist ready for the final strikes. The once beautiful gems were crushed and cracked. His eyes and smile were shining in wicked delight.

Jack pressed his hood buttons with trembling fingers, to reveal his bare face. "You're right, Your Grace, I'm not a killer"—he gestured above with his eyes— "but he is."

Oakenfol frowned and looked upwards. "What? Oh shi—"

The archduke's story ended with a crunch.

CHAPTER 35

The tempest evaporated soon after Oakenfol's demise.

Jack found Annabelle's chambers, guarded by a dozen men. Swords, spears, muskets; they were aimed with quaking arms and strained eyes.

"The archduke is dead. So is the Red Nightmare." He pointed at the door behind them. "The princess is going to be your new queen; I can assure you. Drop your weapons. The battle is over."

The guards glanced at each other in silence. Their weapons remained readied.

He flexed his metal fists. "Either your weapons or your blood will be on that floor. Choose."

Steel and wood clattered and clunked on stone. The soldiers raised hands in surrender. Jack unlocked the door to find Annabelle perched on her four-poster bed, unharmed. She ran and hugged him, then stepped back, snout gaping, eyes wide and ears sticking straight up. "What happened to you? You're all steel?"

"Titanium, not that it matters now. Annabelle, your father."

"He's gone, isn't he?"

"Yes. I'm sorry it had to turn out like this."

"Did you…?"

"No. I don't have it in me, and I'm glad to say that."

Liquid welled in her amber eyes. "It had to happen. I'm still sad though. You must think I'm stupid."

"Of course not. He was still your father, no matter what he did. Don't ever apologize for being a kind-hearted person, ok?"

She stepped back into his embrace, weeping. "If he had lived, you wouldn't have. So, I'm both sad and glad. Was it at least quick?"

"Very. He didn't suffer." Much.

"How did he—never mind, I can't bear to think about it. And Chikara?"

"He's history. He's the Red Dead Nightmare now."

"How did you—"

"I'll explain later. For now, do you have any idea where my painting kit would be? I need to patch up a friend and then tomorrow, after I've gotten some much needed sleep, I have a surprise for you."

* * *

His painting kit was laid out in full, on a rock by the lakeside. Annabelle was sitting in a comfortable chair with shallows lapping near her slipper-clad feet, the sun's rays wrapped around her silvery silk dress in warm embrace. The lake was her favourite place, so it seemed a fitting location.

Samonoska, now restored, glided and flapped in broad circles, far above. Jack was also back to his regular self, not a speck of metal to be seen. He'd brushed his clothes brand new too. For the special occasion about to take place.

He rolled and folded his sweater sleeves to elbow level, not wanting any interference from material while he worked.

"Your arms, they're all scarred," said Annabelle in concern.

"It's ok, I deserve them, believe me. I'm alive, that's all that matters. And I've got more important considerations right now. Do you have a particular kind of bird you like to listen to?"

"Bird?"

"Yes, we need some music for this grand occasion. I thought birdsong would be an appropriate choice."

"I don't know. Any of them? All of them? You choose."

"Ok, let me try something new." He dripped black paint in his palm and squeezed it tight. Wishing hard, he released his open palm into the air. "Blackbirds!"

Floods of blackbirds streamed from his hand in a cloud of contended chirps. They rested on the rocks, and trees, singing their new-born chorus, much to the delight of Annabelle. "Wonderful! How about nightingales?"

Jack did the same again with brown. "Nightingales!" They fluttered forth in an eruption of exquisite song. One came to rest on Annabelle's hand, warbling, curious, making her eyes shine in amazement. "It's incredible! What a delightful surprise, this is all so lovely, Jack."

"That's not the surprise."

"What do you mean? Then what is?"

"Do you trust me?"

Her tone sharpened a fraction, as she feigned annoyance. "Of course, silly."

He picked up one of the smaller brushes, running his finger across its silky tip. Nightingales and blackbirds sang in harmony as the lake's gentle ripples glimmered with sunshine. He sighed, staring at the tiny bristles. "All this time I've still been an apprentice."

"Oh, come on, you can't be an apprentice,

surely. Not with these powers. You created a griffin for goodness' sake."

He nodded. "I've been an apprentice. But today, I think that's finally going to change. Annabelle, I'm not sure of a subtle way to ask this, so I'll just be direct: would you like me to make your face normal?"

"Yes. Yes, please." Her answer was rushed, shaken out in trembling words as she perched forward in her chair. "But I'm scared. What if—"

"If you give me your trust, I won't let you down."

She looked at the chirping birds surrounding her. "I trust you"—she grazed fingertips along her furry snout, nodding— "use your powers."

He dripped white and red on the palette, mixing them. Then, standing with the coated brush in hand, he approached Annabelle.

"Today I make my masterpiece."

✣ ✣ ✣

Sunbeams. Breeze. Birdsong. The lake was a haven of love and calm.

Jack used every brush in his kit. The tiny ones for finest detail, up to the largest for broad strokes across the collarbone, throat and neck.

"It tickles. Feels funny," said Annabelle with a light tremble in her tone.

"Are you ok?"

"Oh yes, I'm fine. It's just a little scary. I, um, I—I can't see my nose anymore." She looked downwards. "There's no fur either."

"Don't worry, I know what I'm doing. Your nose is still there, just different."

"Different how?"

"You'll see. Have a little patience"—he bowed his head cheekily— "Your Grace."

Her tongue jutted an inch, in mock defiance. "I can't see my tongue either!"

"Calm down, Annabelle. Everything's going to be fine, I promise."

Eventually, Jack stood back. Observing, scrutinizing. "Ok. I think we're done. Want to see?"

She tutted, shuffling in rustles of frills and silk. "Any more silly questions?"

He laughed. Taking the largest brush, he painted a gleaming oval mirror. "Are you ready?"

She took a deep breath. "Yes."

He turned the mirror. "Welcome to the new you. Welcome to your new life, Annabelle, Queen of all the Known Lands."

She gaped. Her eyes—a subtle blend of emerald and auburn—flared in disbelief. She rubbed the smooth toffee skin of her high cheekbones, where fur had once coated. Cascades of hazelnut hair floated down her shoulders in sumptuous curls. Snout was now pink pout and button nose. Her furry ears had changed to delicate shells of perfection.

Annabelle was a wonder to behold. The most beautiful woman in the Known Lands.

The birds warbled their approval in unison. Even the lake's surface seemed to quiver a little quicker.

"It's me? It's me! It can't be me? I—I'm beautiful? I'm beautiful!" She leapt from her chair and huddled into him; her silky curls burrowed against his neck. "I'm beautiful, thanks to you! Thank you! Thank you!"

Jack smiled and kissed her hazel crown. "You always were beautiful. I just brought what was inside to the surface."

CHAPTER 36

Queen Annabelle was on her throne.

She'd had the lion and leopard leather removed. It was now upholstered in golden satin and green velvet. A stunning chair. Plain-looking compared to the lady sitting on it.

Jack was standing on the step nearest to her. The battle had been won, but bittersweet emotions still bombarded. He'd stayed to help with the clean-up, but now it was time to leave.

"But why do you have to go? Why not stay here with me?" Her irises—like exotic diamonds—were glistening with liquid, the slender lips quivering.

"Because this is you now"—he gestured down her flawless head and flowing silk dress—"and you'll never grow old and die. This is you, forever. And I—"

"So, then you can stay with me forever." She spoke with defiant tone, but the eyes conceded futility. He'd already told her firmly he had to leave.

Shaking his head softly, he said, "You'll never grow old and die. And I envy you."

She leaned forward, the porcelain skin around her eyes folding in tiny crinkles. "Envy me? Why? What do you mean?"

Jack blew a long sigh. "Because I will die, Annabelle." He stepped closer and squeezed her delicate hand. "As sure, as you're the most beautiful woman in this world. I will grow old, and I will die. You won't."

Her grip shifted tightly, clasping her palm in his. She smelled of faint lavender and lemon zest. "How do you know? Maybe you're wrong? How can you do all these incredible things, and you die, but I don't? That's crazy! It doesn't make any sense."

He drew the back of her hand to his lips and planted a gentle kiss, mixing smile and grimace. "I've abandoned trying to judge what's crazy and what isn't. All I know is, my father, Dante De Luca, was right about everything. All the things he told me, warned me about, tried to protect me from. He was right every time. I know he's right about this too. I won't ignore his wisdom again. My heart has a limited number of beats, no matter where I am. It's a fact. A cruel one, but it doesn't reduce its truth."

She stared at the red carpet stretching down the steps. "And you're absolutely sure I can't come with you, through your—what did you call it?"

"Portal. Absolutely sure. And don't you ever try to go through it, ok? Promise me." He pressed his palm against hers, speaking in solid tone.

"I promise."

"In fact, I think I'm going to try my best to seal it before I go. It's dangerous. Please never ever let anyone go within even a mile of it, ok?"

"Seal it? Does that mean you won't even come back and visit sometimes?"

"It has to be a clean break. I don't want you to see me a little bit older every visit, until I become an old man. More decrepit each time, greyer and wrinklier, and then, eventually, I don't visit at all. Do you want that?"

Annabelle beckoned and he bent. She kissed his cheek; the firm press of her lips sending tingles across his body. "No. You've made my life heaven. I couldn't suffer that hell."

"I couldn't bear to see you suffer either. Or for you to see me old." Gently releasing her hand, he stood straight and flicked his raven fringe. "You're only used to young and gorgeous Jack, after all."

Annabelle smiled, her striking eyes under liquid strain. "You'd still be handsome to me, old man or not. But yes, I understand."

"By the way, what will you do with Berenza

and his squad?"

Her voice sharpened a fraction. "Exile, beyond the Titans. They can take food and water, no weapons. They'll stay in the dungeon for now. Hugo's keeping them company. In a cell of his own. He'll be going too."

"And if they return?"

"They'll have to discuss their trespass with Samonoska."

Jack smiled. "He's a keeper then? I was worried he might scare you."

"Not at all. We've taken quite a shine to each other, in fact. He's very protective of me. I get the keen sense he wants to stay close by my side. Besides, my people are used to having a griffin guarding Oakenfol Castle. It'll just be a good one now, instead."

"Good, I'm glad he's happy here with you. I'll be sad never to see him again, but I'll feel better knowing he's here, watching over you. Keeping you safe."

It was time. Jack placed the painting kit's leather strap across his shoulder, adjusting it snug under his elbow. He walked down the steps and stood looking in admiration of Queen Annabelle. "This is farewell, dear Annabelle."

Her voice was trembling, stuttering over the words. "This is indeed farewell, but you'll always have a place in my heart."

"And you in mine. And don't be sad"—he pointed around the opulent throne room with palm tips— "you have eternity."

Gripping the arms of the massive throne, she spoke with a straightened back and stony tone. "I am a queen"—tears streamed down her flawless cheeks— "and I will be sad if I want to, thank you very much."

Jack smiled and bowed. "As you command, Your Grace."

"Farewell, my dear Jack."

CHAPTER 37

Samonoska soared, heading back towards Oakenfol Castle with a farewell screech.

Jack watched the King of the Griffin's mighty wings flap for the last time. His sweater and fringe fluttered from the gusts. Their final flight had been brief but filled with affection. A tender memory to be treasured all his days.

Painting a path through the toppled cedar trees to reach the portal, he re-sealed the route behind him with each few steps. Fizzing rays engulfed him in brief, brilliant dazzle as he climbed into the light.

And there he was. Back in the Gallery of Galleries. The automatic lighting flickered on as soon as his feet stepped from the canvas onto the gallery floor.

Everything was the same. There was nothing but thousands of paintings and wafts of vanilla wood polish. He stood in silence, staring at The Lands of Queen Annabelle. That's what he'd decided to rename it.

It was like he'd never even been in the damn thing. The canvas' details all looked identical to when he'd entered. After all the things he'd been through, how incred—one thing had changed. The blue crackles had ceased. He stood for twenty minutes to be sure. Yes, they'd stopped. He hoped that meant the end of tempests for Annabelle's world.

He wished her nothing but happiness for all eternity.

Looking at Samonoska's painting, he saw the mountains, forests, meadows, valleys, a sea. No griffin. As suspected, he hadn't imitated his friend, he'd transported him, somehow.

And now he wouldn't see him again. Sighing at the nasty scars wound around his forearms and across his palm, he reminded himself these were the prices to be paid for arrogance and stupidity. He would be mindful of avoiding similar expenses in the future.

Jack walked through the gallery and up its tunnel to the marble and brass beyond.

EPILOGUE

"Yes, come in!" Jack knew it was Dante from his three soft knocks.

Caramel wrinkles and grey curls peeked round the door. "Good morning, apprentice. How did you sleep?"

"Great, thanks! What are we doing today?"

"How about a little trip across the sky?"

"Samonoska!" Jolts of excitement sprung him from bed in superhero pyjamas.

Dante chuckled. "Maybe at the weekend if you study hard in your lessons. No, today we will use more conventional means to fly. Come on, get dressed and let's have breakfast, then you can try something different. See you in the breakfast room. And be quick, young man."

After a hurried breakfast of crunched toast and glugged orange juice, they walked through broad corridors of polished brass and gleaming marble, to one of the largest lawns. A blue and white helicopter was waiting. The blades began whirling, whisking wind across the manicured grass in waves. Dante clasped Jack's hand in his leathery palm. His beard and hair flapping, he shouted, "If you can ride a griffin, this will be easy, don't worry." He slid the chunky door across in a rasping glide and helped Jack inside, closing it again with a heavy clunk.

Dante strapped Jack into one side of a double leather seat. The straps were snug but comfy. Then he did the same for himself. He was wearing one of his paint spattered black sweater and trouser outfits. Jack giggled to himself and wondered if all those clothes would be worth a lot because they were—kind of—painted by Dante De Luca.

There were big tins of paint, of assorted colours, stacked in the cabin area. Far too many. Jack was ok, but Dante's longer legs were knocking against the stack. The paint wasn't like the type he'd been learning to use on canvas. It was for painting walls and stuff like that.

"Where are we going?" They were huddled close, but he still had to speak louder because of the rotor's whirring.

"The west coast. To a Scottish prince's estate."

"Wow! A real prince?"

Dante flicked his eyebrows and smiled with

soft slyness. "Yes, like in the fairy tales." He gave a thumbs up to the pilot, who was sitting behind a half-wall of leather and glass. "He wants me to make him some"—his eyes weaved, searching—"speciality art."

Jack peered out the window. The ground got smaller, then he could see the whole palace, as they rose higher and higher. He still couldn't believe he was lucky enough to live there. With the coolest grownup in the world.

The helicopter was banking gently, he could see towns and villages passing underneath in rows, circles and squares of tiny orange and brown roofs. The pilot looked so cool in his navy uniform and sunglasses, and those things pilots wore over their ears.

"Jack, have you ever heard of an artist named Jackson Pollock?"

He shrugged. "Sorry. Is he famous?"

Dante nodded. "Was, yes. One of the most famous of modern times."

"Oh, why's that? Could he paint like us?"

He shook his sheep curls in modest bobs. "Not like us in terms of making worlds, but he was brilliant in his own way. He had a method, an interesting one called action painting."

"Action painting? What's that?"

Dante gestured with eyes. "What do you see in this cabin?"

The answer was easy. "Paint."

"Yes, and what don't you see?"

Jack shrugged. "Maybe, paintbrushes?"

Dante rubbed a gentle palm over Jack's raven locks. "Exactly, paintbrushes. Bravo. Why paint and no paintbrushes?"

"It's for decorating, not doing pictures?"

The grey curls bunched. Chuckles wafted sweet tobacco and spearmint. "In a way, yes. Action painting uses no brush. The paint is dribbled, splashed and smeared. You can fling it all over the place."

"Fling it? But that's not real painting."

Eyes widening, he jerked his neck back and asked, "If the painting comes alive, what does it matter how it is constructed?"

Throwing paint around as you felt like it, that wasn't the same as real painting. Because anybody could do that. "It just seems like a waste of paint if you ask me."

Dante pursed his lips and nodded. Then he took a deep breath, exhaling slowly. He finished with a smile. "And?"

Jack shrugged. "And what?"

"Was that a waste?"

"A waste of what?"

"Oxygen."

"Of course not. We need oxygen to live."

Dante leaned close, his shoulder pressing gently against Jack's. "And some people need art to feel alive too. Paint can never be wasted if it is used in a way that contributes to happy life." He craned his neck, eyes smiling. "Oh, and here we are."

"What are we here for? What does the prince want?"

"For me to make art, from above"—he pointed at the helicopter's swaying window—"on a patch of tarmac down there."

"Make art from all the way up here? That's impossible!"

Dante pinched his cheek softly. "Impossible? This, from the boy who rides the King of the Griffins through the starry sky."

Well, ok, that did make Jack sound pretty cool. "Ok, maybe it's possible, but I can't see how? You don't even have a canvas. Tarmac isn't canvas."

"Yes, it is, in this case."

The grooved metal floor was wobbling a little as the helicopter hovered. Dante unclicked himself from the chunky straps and fitted a much thicker strap around his waist, attaching it with a rope to a thick metal bar, using one of those funny big clips that looked like a giant nappy pin.

"What's that?"

"A safety harness. Can I help you put one on?"

Jack clutched fingertips round his firm chair straps. They were solid, safe. He looked out the window at the ground. They were still quite far up. He was curling his lips, gritting teeth. "Will I have to go near the edge when you open the doors?"

"Yes, right on the edge, but it's safe. Don't worry. I'd never let anything happen to you."

A minute later, Jack was belted in the thick leather strap and attached with rope, like Dante. But his stomach and nerves were rebelling. This was scarier than riding Samonoska; he couldn't crash. "I feel a little scared. I think I can't do it, I'm sorry Dante."

"You don't have to be sorry. I know it's scary, but I'll make you a deal. Care to listen?

"Ok." Dante's deals were good.

"You sit on the edge and help me make art, and I'll give you a share from the prince's fee."

"Fair share?"

"Mama Mia!" Dante was speaking in Italian, waving his hands in the air, in mock anger, as if offended by the question.

Jack's giggles pushed his nerves to the side. "Ok, ok, deal."

Dante slid the doors open. The wind washed in and the rotor's sound strengthened. Jack was shaking, peering at the patch of tarmac far below. It was probably quite big, but within the massive field, it looked tiny.

Dante grasped a tin's plastic semi-circular handle, pulled it to the edge and pried its top with a chisel. It popped off to reveal gloopy blue. He lifted it across to Jack, who held its bulky container between skinny thighs. Dante did the same for himself, except the tin's contents were red.

They both perched on the cabin's edge. Dante's legs dangling above green meadows, Jack's in squat, glancing back every few minutes to check the attachment was still ok.

"Dante, now what do we do?"

"Well,"—he lifted his tin with one hand curled inside the rim, among the paint, the thick liquid seeping between his knuckles— "we fling it down there. In your case, tip the can, it's enough."

Dante shook the whole tin of red onto the tarmac patch and Jack watched with awe. It landed with a splat, spraying in wide radius. "Wow! You got almost all of it on the patch!"

He clanked it aside and opened another tin with soft clunk. "Then you try for all of it this time. Go on, try, Jack, it's fun"—he tapped the rim of Jack's tin twice— "tip it right over, go on."

And so, he did. His fingers coated in gooey blue drips, he peered cautiously. He'd scored a near perfect hit! The paint had splattered in the square's middle. Just a few splashes had reached the surrounding lawn.

Jack was giggling more with every tin. He even tried dribbling the paint in circles and stripes as his confidence in the safety harness grew. Dante stood, tumbling and flaying with focus then, for some tins, casually tipping like Jack, without care at all.

What Jack realised was if you were as famous as Dante, people paid you for any kind of art. It was weird, like the name meant more than the effort. It was great fun though. Jack smiled as Dante flung the contents of the final tin and said, "Ok, our creation is complete. Let's go back."

The helicopter didn't even land.

"And the prince is going to pay you for that?" Jack was still in shock that a prince—a real prince—would pay for paint to be spattered all over a patch of tarmac on his grounds.

"A decent fee, yes. I think he intends to cover and preserve it and make an exhibition, but that's his business." Dante was strapped back into his seat, breathing in hard happy gasps with paint speckles increased across his black sweater.

It had been great fun. Pouring paint from a helicopter and being called an artist for it. Dante's life was even cooler than he'd thought.

"So, I can have some of the money, since I helped, right?"

Dante clasped his seat straps. "That was the deal, as I recall. How much do you want?"

"Really?"

"Well, that was the deal, was it not? A fair share. What you think is fair, I will give. So?

Floor wobbled, rotor whirred; eyebrows lowered in feigned contention. They stared at each other with playful smiles. Jack didn't want to be greedy, but he'd try pushing his luck a little. "Hmm a thousand pounds?"

Dante nodded. "Deal."

"Wow, a thousand pounds! I'm rich!!" He paused. "Hold on a mi—could I have had more?"

Dante smiled and shrugged. "Maybe. Aim a little higher next time"—he pinched Jack's cheek tenderly— "you're a master in the making, remember."

The helicopter continued its whirs back towards the palace.

Jack rested his head on Dante's paint-blotched shoulder. "Dante?"

"Yes, dear boy."

"Nah, it's silly, forget it. You might not want to hear it."

"What is silly to one may be deadly serious to another. What is it?"

"Nah, my dad says—"

He flicked his backhand. "What do *you* say?"

Jack looked at the back of pilot's head. His cheeks were feeling hot.

Dante looked at the pilot too, his eyelids narrowing. "How about if you whisper it in my ear, then nobody will hear except me?"

"You might be angry."

"Impossible."

Jack was shy but the emotions were bubbling inside him, rising from his chest and pressing behind his lips. He needed to say it.

The seat straps strained tight against both their chests as Dante tilted his head to the side and Jack leaned close.

Jack formed a shield with his fingers, cupping them around Dante's ear. He'd neither said the words before nor had them said to him. He hoped it wouldn't sound too silly, as he whispered:

"I love you."

ABOUT THE AUTHOR

Alexander Small

Alexander Small is a teacher from Scotland. He had the idea for The Painter's Apprentice while staring at a painting in his bedroom, during the particularly bleak Scottish winter of 2020. He imagined how nice it would be to step into the painting--a country path scene full of greenery and warm sunshine--and walk wherever he wanted within that world.

Alexander enjoys travel, swimming, eating out and writing stories that give people pleasure.

He lives in rural Scotland where the wild haggis roam.

A NOTE ON REVIEWS FROM THE AUTHOR

Dear readers

Thank you so much for taking the time to read my first Young Adult novel, The Painter's Apprentice. I hope you liked it.

Something readers don't always realise is how important reviews are to authors, in order to make sales and continue to support themselves financially.

They're incredibly important though.

If you could please take a few minutes of your time to leave a review on the website you purchased your copy from, I would be extremely grateful.

Warm thanks

Alexander Small

SEQUEL

Jack will be back!

His next adventure, The Painter's Promise, is coming soon!

For updates, teasers, freebies and more, sign up to Alexander's newletter at the link below:

https://mailchi.mp/1e3e44441673/alexander-small-landing-page

Please feel free to like Alexander's Facebook page at:

https://www.facebook.com/alexanders-mall2020

You can also reach him via email at:

alexandersmallauthor@gmail.com

Printed in Great Britain
by Amazon